Starscape Books by David Lubar

NOVELS

Flip

My Rotten Life: Nathan Abercrombie, Accidental Zombie, Book One

Hidden Talents

True Talents

STORY COLLECTIONS

The Battle of the Red Hot Pepper Weenies
and Other Warped and Creepy Tales

The Curse of the Campfire Weenies
and Other Warped and Creepy Tales

In the Land of the Lawn Weenies
and Other Warped and Creepy Tales

Invasion of the Road Weenies
and Other Warped and Creepy Tales

Nathan Abercrombie,
Accidental Zombie
BOOK TWO

DEAD
GUY
SPY

David Lubar

A Tom Doherty Associates Book · New York

DEAD GUY SPY

Copyright © 2009 by David Lubar

Goop Soup excerpt copyright © 2009 by David Lubar

Reader's Guide copyright © 2009 by Tor Books

A Starscape Book
Published by Tom Doherty Associates, LLC
175 Fifth Avenue
New York, NY 10010

www.tor-forge.com

Tor® is a registered trademark of Tom Doherty Associates, LLC.

Library of Congress Cataloging-in-Publication Data

Lubar, David.
    Dead guy spy / David Lubar.—1st ed.
        p. cm.
    "A Starscape Book."
    Summary: When fifth-grader Nathan Abercrombie, a half-dead zombie whose body cannot heal itself, is approached by messengers from the Bureau of Useful Misadventures (B.U.M.) and offered the chance for a cure if he will become a spy, he does not realize that B.U.M. is not exactly trustworthy.
    ISBN 978-0-7653-1635-6 (hardcover)
    ISBN 978-0-7653-2507-5 (trade paperback)
    [1. Zombies—Fiction. 2. Spies—Fiction. 3. Wrestling—Fiction.
    4. Schools—Fiction.]   I. Title.
    PZ7.L96775De 2010
    [Fic]—dc22

                                                                    2009036337

First Edition: January 2010

Printed in December 2009 in the United States of America by RR Donnelley, Harrisonburg, Virginia

0   9   8   7   6   5   4   3   2   1

For Masae Namba, aka "Auntie,"
who keeps me supplied with lemons and good wishes

CONTENTS

▼

INTRODUCTION

▼

I used to think secret agents were these awesome guys who drove fast cars, wore expensive clothes, and practiced deadly karate. Now I know better.

Bushwhacked!

It's pretty creepy when some stranger follows you, spies on you, and tries to discover the deep, dark, half-cool, half-rotten secret that only your two closest friends in the world know about. It's even creepier when it happens three times in one day.

It all started Monday morning, when Mookie and I were walking to school. He'd stayed over that weekend because his parents had won a free dinner at a restaurant in Vermont. Since we lived in New Jersey, it took them a while to get up there.

"I hope they bring me maple syrup," Mookie said as we headed out the door. "It's not just good for pancakes, you know. It's awesome on everything. Even chicken wings."

"I think I'd pick hot sauce," I said. "Not that I'll ever eat wings again."

Food didn't play a big part in my life—or death—these days. Anything I swallowed just stayed in my stomach and slowly rotted.

"Hey, there's no law that says you have to stick with one sauce. You can mix them. That's half the fun. Chocolate syrup and mustard are awesome on pretzels. I'd bet maple syrup and hot sauce would be great together. Sweet and spicy—yummmm."

He closed his eyes, spun around, and made chewing sounds. The chews turned into a "gaaaahhh!" when he tripped on his laces. The "gaaaahhh!" ended with a crash as he slammed into a couple metal garbage cans at the end of a driveway, spilling out a mess of leftover food, crumpled paper, and these large gray lumps that might have been cat litter.

I went to help put the garbage back. That stuff doesn't bother me. I can stick my face three inches from the grossest pile of week-old road kill without feeling a quiver in my gut.

Mookie had a pretty strong stomach, too. I'd seen him eat things that would make a cockroach puke. Once, he chomped down on a pickle he'd coated with strawberry jelly and dipped in crumbled fish sticks, just to gross out some girls at another lunch table.

But this stuff was making him gag. So I took care of the mess while he stood next to me and talked about the weirder and sloppier pieces.

"Whoa, that looks like pig intestines."

"I really hope that's just chocolate pudding."

"Ick—who'd throw away that much oatmeal?"

"Oh, man—I think that's a diaper."

I finished up, then wiped my hands in the grass. "That's weird," Mookie said as he put the lids on the cans. "I don't remember that bush."

"What bush?"

"By the blue house." He pointed back the way we'd come. "See that bush by the corner? It wasn't there before."

"So what. Maybe it's new. People are always planting things around here. Come on. Let's get going."

Mookie kept glancing over his shoulder as we walked. "Ever feel like you're being followed?"

"Only when you're behind me." I grabbed his arm and yanked him toward the school. Mookie got distracted pretty easily. Walking with him usually meant I did a lot of waiting up. Or backing up. Or grabbing and yanking. And a bit of picking up, since this wasn't the first time in his life he'd crashed into stuff. I figure he wipes out about five garbage cans on an average week. If people ever turned into objects, Mookie would become a bowling ball.

"No, not like that. I mean secretly followed, like by someone who doesn't want you to know he's there." He turned around again. "Whoa!"

"What?" I really didn't want to stand around talking. We were going to be late for school if he kept this up.

He grabbed my shoulder. "The bush moved."

13

"Knock it off."

"Really," Mookie said. "Seriously. I think it's following us."

"Bushes don't move."

"Right. And dead kids don't walk."

Okay, he had a point there. You could sort of call me dead. Or half-dead.

I'd accidentally gotten splashed with a whole jar of Hurt-Be-Gone by my friend Abigail's crazy uncle Zardo. The formula was supposed to remove bad feelings. The problem was, he'd used one wrong ingredient. Yeah—just one. But it was enough to change my life, big time.

Now, I didn't have a pulse or heartbeat. I didn't feel pain. I didn't need to breathe. But I could walk, talk, and think. It's not as bad as it sounds. I could do some pretty cool things. Maybe even some brave things.

Mookie liked to call me a zombie. I didn't totally agree with that, but I definitely couldn't explain how I was able to pass for a living kid. If I could walk, I guess a bush could move. I turned and looked.

"Whoa!"

The bush was less than a block away. I stared at it, waiting to see if it would move again. It just sat there, quivering in the light breeze. But there was no doubt it had moved. Mookie was right. We were being followed.

2

Leaf Me Alone

I walked toward the corner.

"What are you doing?" Mookie yelled after me.

"Finding out what's going on," I said.

"Be careful, it might attack you! I've read all these books where people get killed in the African bush."

"I don't think it's the bushes that kill them. I think it's lions or something."

I wasn't worried. The bush had floppy branches that drooped all the way to the ground, and tiny green leaves. There was nothing deadly about it. As I got closer, the bush started to inch backwards, like it was trying to move without looking like it was moving. I dashed forward.

"Yipes!" The cry came from behind the bush. A man

tumbled backward, landing on his butt on the sidewalk. I guess he was trying to drag the bush and lost his grip.

That's really strange, I thought as I got a good look at him. He was wearing a green flannel shirt, green corduroy pants, green gloves, green shoes, green socks, and a green wool cap pulled low over his forehead—exactly what someone would wear if he was trying to blend in with a bush. He looked pretty tall, though it was hard to tell for sure, since he was sprawled on the ground. He had red hair, big ears, and green eyes. If he'd been about three feet shorter, I would have asked him for his pot of gold.

Instead, I asked him something a lot more important. "Why are you following me?"

The man stood up and dusted his pants off. "What an absurd question. I am not following you. Should I be following you?"

He had an English accent, like the people in those infomercials who are trying to sound classy while they sell mops, vacuum cleaners, and grilled-cheese makers.

"Is there anything that makes you followable? Are you expecting to be followed? Hmmmm?"

"No . . ."

"Well, there you go. I certainly wouldn't be following you, then. Would I?"

"Why are you dressed in green?"

"I'm Irish."

"You sound British."

"And you sound childish." He leaned over and grabbed

the bush. "If you must know, I am taking my new plant home."

I walked down this street every day on the way to school. I didn't recognize this guy. But I wasn't going to waste time thinking about it. There was no reason not to believe him. He could have just moved in. I'd actually be a lot happier believing he wasn't following me. The last thing I wanted was attention, especially now that I was working on a top-secret plan to do something really cool with my zombie powers.

"Okay. Sorry I made you fall."

"I didn't fall. I have excellent reflexes. I was merely resting."

"Whatever." I trotted back to Mookie. "He's taking his new plant home. And he has excellent reflexes."

"This town is getting weirder and weirder," Mookie said.

We reached school without running into any more traveling plants.

Abigail was waiting for us by the front entrance. We'd only been friends for a little while, but we'd been through a lot during that time.

"Hi, guys." She was still treating me special for saving her life, but I figured she'd get over it in another week or two. She had so many things racing through her mind, I'd bet that the old thoughts kept getting shoved out to make room for new ones.

She reached for my backpack. "Can I carry that for you?"

I stepped away from her. "I'm fine. It's not heavy."

"I know," she said. "But you need to be careful not to strain anything. Your body can't repair itself."

"I'm careful."

That was the biggest problem with being dead. My body didn't heal. If I broke a finger or a toe, I had to glue it back with a special mixture I'd discovered. And then, for a couple seconds while my nerves flickered back to life, I felt a ton of pain, like my bones and muscles were being forced through a meat grinder. So I was more careful about accidents than most kids. But I wasn't going to stop enjoying my life just because I was dead. If I started to hide from the world, I might as well just crawl into a grave and make friends with the worms.

The bell rang, and we headed to our home base in Room 103. When I dropped my language arts and social studies homework on Ms. Otranto's desk, she looked up from her attendance book and smiled at me. "Thank you, Nathan."

Since I didn't need to sleep, I had plenty of time for homework. Teachers seem to like you a lot more when you do a good job on your assignments.

After social studies, we moved upstairs for science with Ms. Delambre. Instead of desks, we had lab tables and stools, just like the big kids had in Lonchan Middle School. Mookie and I used to sit by ourselves at a table near the window, but after we became friends with Abigail, she joined us.

Ms. Delambre pointed to a box of gears and pulleys.

"We're going to be experimenting with mechanical advantages today."

My eyes drifted toward the window. I'd already read the gears-and-pulleys chapter in our textbook. I wasn't a science genius like Abigail, but I pretty much understood the lesson, so I knew what Ms. Delambre was going to say. For a moment, as my mind wandered, I didn't really look at anything in particular. Then, when I realized what I was seeing, I yelped and nearly toppled off my stool.

"Whoa!"

Ms. Delambre stopped in the middle of her sentence and stared at our table. "Is there a problem, Nathan?"

"No. Sorry." I scrunched my stool back toward the table and tried to stare ahead. But I couldn't resist the urge to get a better look. As soon as I could, I snuck another glance out the window.

It hadn't been my imagination. There was a squirrel on top of a phone pole by the road, twenty or thirty feet away from the window. He was holding something the size of a large walnut. That wouldn't have made me shout, except for one thing. The squirrel wasn't getting ready to eat his lunch. This walnut had a tiny red light on it and a shiny lens. And it was aimed right at me.

"He's got a squirrel-cam!" I gasped.

3

I Scope Not

Ms. Delambre shot me another glare. I clamped my mouth shut until she looked away. Then I smacked Mookie on the leg to get his attention.

"What's wrong?" he whispered out of the side of his mouth.

I jerked my head toward the window, trying to get him to look that way.

"You have a twitch?" he asked. "Stiff neck?"

"Muscle spasm?" Abigail asked. "That's peculiar. I wouldn't expect dead muscles to twitch, unless they were exposed to an electric current."

"No!" I snarled the word through gritted teeth, then pointed out the window. "Over there . . ."

Mookie and Abigail looked.

"What?" they both asked.

"That squirrel has a miniature camera," I said.

Mookie squinted through his glasses, scrunching up his forehead. "Come on. That's just a walnut."

"No way. Why would a squirrel hold a walnut up to his eyes?" I asked.

"So he could admire it?" Mookie said.

"Hutner! Nathan! Abigail! Do I have to separate the three of you?" Ms. Delambre always called Mookie by his real name, even though he begged her not to. His parents had planned to name him Hunter, but they'd messed up when they'd filled out his birth certificate.

"No. Sorry." I waited until she finished explaining the experiment. When she started handing out the gears, I checked the window again. The squirrel was still there, and the camera was still aimed at me.

As soon as we started setting up our experiment, and kids at all the tables were talking, I said, "I'm sure it's a camera. I need to get a closer look."

"Too bad there's no telescope in here," Mookie said.

Abigail stared up at the ceiling, which told me she was thinking. Then she snapped her fingers. "Got it!" She pointed to one of the bins on the counter along the side wall, right past the sink. "Mookie, can you spill something into the red bin? The one with all the lenses."

He turned toward the back of the room, then nodded, grabbed his pencil, and hopped off his stool. "I was born to spill."

When he reached the sharpener, he started cranking away. "Hey—it's full. I'll empty it." He pulled off the container and sprinted for the wastebasket.

When Mookie got near the red bin, he tripped on his loose sneaker lace—on purpose, for once—and lost his grip on the container. Shavings went flying. A bunch of them spilled onto the lenses.

"Hutner, get back in your seat," Ms. Delambre said.

"That was fun," Mookie whispered as he climbed on his stool. "I love spilling things."

"What a mess," Ms. Delambre said. She headed toward the back of the room.

I still had no idea what was going on.

"I'll clean it!" Abigail leaped up and dashed toward the counter.

"Thank you, Abigail," Ms. Delambre said. "That's very thoughtful."

After Abigail brushed off all the shavings, she took the lenses to the sink and washed them. That didn't seem necessary, but I'd learned a while back that Abigail never did anything without a reason.

She pulled a brown paper towel from the dispenser and held it up. "Ms. Delambre," she called. "These are pretty rough. Will they scratch the lenses?"

"There are some rolls of softer towels in the closet," Ms. Delambre said.

22

I saw Abigail smile as she went to the closet. After she dried the lenses, she stuck one into an end of the paper towel tube. She took a smaller lens, wrapped the outside with used paper towels, and crammed it in the other end of the tube.

After she put the rest of the lenses back, she brought the tube over to our table. "Go distract Ms. Delambre," Abigail told Mookie.

"I'm the man for the job." He walked over to Ms. Delambre's desk and held up a gear. "Does this look round to you? Gears are supposed to be round, right? But this one sort of looks kind of oval. Will it still work if it's oval? If not, can I swap it for a round one? Besides, some of the teeth aren't as pointy as the others. Do they all need the same amount of pointyness?"

I had a feeling Ms. Delambre was going to be distracted for a while.

Abigail handed me the tube. "I made a telescope. I had to estimate the focal length, but it should be close enough. Take a look."

I stared at her. I didn't know you could make a telescope that easily.

"Hurry," she said. "The squirrel could climb down at any moment."

I held up the tube and took a look. "Hey, everything is upside down."

"Of course," Abigail said. "The lenses invert—oh, never mind. Just look."

I looked. Everything wasn't just upside down. It was

also a whole lot closer. If I'd been able to get goose bumps, I definitely would have gotten them now. Close up, there was no doubt. The squirrel wasn't holding a walnut.

I was right. "It's a squirrel-cam."

"That's trouble," Abigail said. "Someone is spying on you."

Squirreled Away

"Why would anyone want to spy on me?"

That didn't make sense. I handed Abigail the telescope. Before she could use it, the squirrel fell off the pole. I ran to the window and looked out.

The squirrel was on its side on the ground next to the pole. It got up and staggered a couple steps. Sparks shot out from under its tail.

Sparks?

It took a couple more steps. Little puffs of smoke drifted from its ears. Then more sparks. Its fur caught fire.

The squirrel exploded.

Shiny parts bounced across the road. It was some sort

of machine! As I watched, a car ran over one of the pieces.

"Nathan!"

Ms. Delambre pointed at my seat. I slunk back. Abigail, Mookie, and I didn't get a chance to talk any more during science. Every time we tried, Ms. Delambre flashed us that steamed look that's a sign she's in danger of overloading. An exploding teacher is a lot more dangerous than an exploding squirrel.

I decided it would be safer to keep my mouth shut until recess. But I had a feeling my friends weren't the only ones who knew I wasn't a normal boy. That was the only way to explain why someone was suddenly spying on me.

While the rest of the fifth grade played kickball, shot baskets, or chased each other around, I huddled with Mookie and Abigail by the broken seesaws, since nobody would interrupt us there.

"Somebody knows I'm a zombie," I said. "You've seen the movies. People don't like to hang out with zombies. All they do is run from them and scream."

Abigail patted my shoulder. "You have no reason to panic. All we really know is that someone is watching you. It's a good idea to gather all available facts before forming a conclusion."

"Someone knows about me. That's a fact." I hated the idea that a stranger had discovered my secret, especially now that I was working on an idea where I needed to totally hide my true identity from the world. I wasn't even ready to share my idea with my friends yet.

26

Abigail shook her head. "Maybe not. Maybe they just suspect something. If they already knew your secret, they wouldn't need to spy on you, would they?"

"I guess that makes sense," I said. "But how could they even know anything?"

Abigail plopped down on the end of a seesaw. "I'm not sure. But the police found Uncle Zardo right after he spilled the zombie formula on you. You were there when he got arrested. Uncle Zardo used to tell me that people were always spying on him. I never paid much attention to that. But I'm beginning to wonder whether there was some truth to it."

"And you're on the computer all night," Mookie said. "My dad told me they can trace everything you do on the computer. That's why he didn't want us to ever get one. But Mom talked him into it, because it makes shopping so much easier. She's always winning stuff online. Like that dinner in Vermont, or the year's supply of goldfish food. If we ever get a fish tank, we're all set."

"The computer?" I thought about how much time I spent online. Even after I did my homework and read ahead in the textbooks, I still had a ton of time to kill at night. It's amazing how long an hour lasts when you're lying in bed and you know you won't fall asleep. So I'd been playing games. But I didn't see how anyone could spy on me that way. Zillions of people played games.

"Whatever you do," Abigail said, "just assume you're being watched. It would be best if you didn't go online at all."

"But I'm playing this really cool vampire game," I said. "I'm up to level forty-two."

"Nathan, the game can wait," Abigail said. "Don't go online. Don't do anything unusual at all. You need to be careful until we find out who's following you and what they're trying to learn."

"I'll be careful." I'd already learned to watch how I acted. Since I didn't need to breathe, I never noticed stinky stuff unless I sniffed on purpose. If everyone else was choking and gagging because of a bad smell—which you could sort of count on happening pretty often if you hung out around Mookie—I had to act like I was choking, too.

Or if someone flicked my ear, I had to pretend it hurt. Since the school had several champion ear flickers, including Rodney Mullasco, I needed to stay alert all the time. Rodney had become especially dangerous ever since I messed up his attempt to get Shawna Lanchester to like him. Luckily, he'd never figured out exactly how I'd pulled off that trick.

Speaking of gagging, the bell rang, and we went into the cafeteria for lunch. The choice today, along with the usual sandwiches and salads, was turkey burgers or extra-chunky vegetable soup, which made me glad I didn't need to eat.

As we stood in line, Mookie pointed at the pale, slimy burgers floating in a shallow pool of greasy liquid. "Those look more like a zombie than you." Then he pointed at the soup. "That looks like it's already taken a trip through the digestive system."

"So what are you getting?" I asked.

"Both."

I bought a tuna sandwich. I wasn't going to eat it, but I'd rather not eat a tuna sandwich than not eat a turkey burger.

The other Second Besters—Adam, Denali, Jenny, Jerome, and Armando—were already at our table, along with the group that used to be known as the Doomed. When they joined us, it didn't drag us down to their level, but sort of raised them up a bit. Snail Girl still didn't talk much, and Ferdinand still flinched at everything that came near him, but they acted less like outcasts.

"Hey, it's Yin and Yang," Adam said when we sat down.

"Huh?" Mookie asked.

"A pair of opposites," he said.

"Nate and I aren't opposites," Mookie said. "We're just not like each other in a bunch of ways."

Adam opened his mouth, then shrugged and closed it. Actually, I guess he was the one Second Bester who'd lost some ground, but he didn't know it. Everyone thought he was the second smartest kid in the class. They didn't know Abigail had been hiding her brains ever since she'd gotten teased for being supersmart back when she was little. Adam was actually the third-smartest kid. But the smartest thing I'd figured out was that none of this really mattered. First, second, third, or tenth smartest, Adam was just Adam. I liked him.

29

I unwrapped my sandwich and let it sit on my tray. Nobody noticed that I didn't eat. They were all too busy with their food. Ferdinand opened his sandwich and ate all the tuna with a fork.

Denali pointed at the bread and laughed. "Hey—it's like a bad musical instrument. It's outta tuna!"

"That's nothing." Mookie took a huge bite of his burger, chewed a bit, then, with his mouth still full of food, said, "I'm gobbling a turkey. Gobble gobble!"

"You are what you eat," Denali said.

All through lunch, I kept looking out the cafeteria window, suspecting everyone who went by. Was the old guy walking a poodle really from around here? Was the pizza-delivery guy who stopped at the house across the street actually a spy? Were those birds in the sky really birds?

I had to keep my zombie identity a secret. Not just because I didn't want everyone running away from me. There was another reason. I'd already had two chances to be a hero. I hadn't planned either of them. But they felt wonderful. I remembered the cheering when I won field day, and the faces of the people in the crowd when I'd carried Abigail from the burning house. I wanted to feel that way again. I wanted to be a hero all the time. So I was working on a plan to become a zombie superhero.

The one thing a superhero absolutely has to protect is his secret identity. And, right now, that was the one thing that looked like it was in super danger.

5

Snap the Ball

The best part about skipping lunch was that I didn't have to go to gym with a stomach full of cafeteria food, like I did back when I was alive.

Mr. Lomux had us sit in the bleachers along the side wall of the gym. There was a rolling chalkboard next to him. That was never a good sign. Words weren't his best thing. He was much better with whistles and balls.

"Wrestling . . ." He let the word hang in the air like it had some sort of special power. Then he wrote it on the board. He actually got most of the letters right.

"Wrestling is more than a sport." He stopped and stared at us for a moment. "In East Craven, wrestling is a way of life. We eat, sleep, and breathe wrestling."

"Well, that leaves me out," I whispered to Mookie.

"Too bad they don't fart wrestling," Mookie said. "I'd be a champ."

Mr. Lomux kept talking. "When you get to East Craven High School, you'll have a chance to be a part of one of the best teams in the state—maybe even the whole country—the East Craven Ravens. Only the very best athletes make the cut. It's never too early to start training."

Never too early? We wouldn't be in high school for another four years. We weren't even in middle school yet. I looked around the bleachers. Some of the kids were leaning forward, like they were ready to leap from their seats and start grappling. Rodney pumped his arms like those professional wrestlers do on TV when they're shouting at the camera. Ferdinand and a couple other kids scooted back like they wanted to run away.

Mookie raised his hand.

"What?" Mr. Lomux asked.

"Can we get names?" Mookie asked. "Real wrestlers have cool names. Can we do that? I want to be the Mookasaurus."

Mr. Lomux glared at Mookie for a moment. Five small veins in his head bulged. We could always tell how angry he was by counting the veins. So far, the record was eight. Mookie was dying to see if there was a ninth vein hiding somewhere on that sweaty head.

I thought Mr. Lomux was going to start shouting. But he shook his head and went back to his speech. "We'll be outside today. But the colder weather's coming. Wednesday, we'll start to work on wrestling skills. I wanted to let you know ahead of time, so you could get ready. You might want to put in some extra time at home with your dumbbells."

Mookie started to open his mouth, but I clamped my hand over it. Mr. Lomux wrote SKILLS on the board. "We'll be learning takedowns, practicing escapes, doing drills, and turning you into the pride of East Craven."

He wrote PRIDE, then put down the chalk. "I'm going to lead you to greatness. Our field day victory was only a start."

Oh boy, not that again. Mr. Lomux had floated around with a goofy smile for a couple days after our school beat Perrin Hall Academy. He even bought pizza for the whole fifth grade.

I think he was looking for another victory. I could understand that. But at least we wouldn't have to do any sort of real competition against another school. And, better yet, I wouldn't have to wrestle a monster like Rodney. He probably weighed fifteen or twenty pounds more than I did. Mookie was safe, too. He was shorter than Rodney, but he weighed a lot more.

After Mr. Lomux took attendance, we went outside to play touch football.

"Who do you think he'll match us up with?" Mookie asked as we walked toward the field.

"Maybe I'll get Daniel or Abner." I was one of the lightest kids in the class—and the second skinniest—so there weren't all that many possibilities. "Or Ferdinand. I think he's about my weight." That would be fine with me. I didn't think Ferdinand was capable of snapping my arms off.

Adam pointed at Dilby "the Digger" Parkland. "I think you'll be with him, Mookie."

"Please, no . . . ," Mookie said as we watched Dilby reach down the back of his shorts to fix some sort of wedgie problem. Then he used the same hand to scratch the inside of his nose.

"Better buy some good soap," I said. "The kind that kills germs." Dilby was always digging at some part of his body with one, or both, of his hands.

We joined the rest of our class. Across the field, Shawna and her friends were practicing cheers while they waited for their teacher.

"Why can't we wrestle them?" Mookie asked.

"Because they'd beat us, and we'd go through life humiliated," Adam said. "Girls are a lot tougher than they look."

"They'd hurt us, for sure," Ferdinand said.

I noticed Abigail standing off to the side, watching the other girls. She was probably tougher than any of them.

When we chose sides for football, I got picked pretty early. Compared with how I used to always be picked last, this was almost a miracle. Everyone still thought I was a great athlete because I'd won field day by doing 239 chin-ups. I can do chin-ups all day. My muscles might be dead, but they never feel tired.

I figured that as long as I didn't totally mess up, or leave a couple body parts on the field, they'd keep believing that for a while. And maybe I was a better athlete than I thought. Our team won. I actually helped make two or three plays.

"Forget wrestling," Mookie said as we walked off the field. "I need to practice football. I keep dropping passes."

"We can toss the ball around after school," I said. I didn't like gym, because Mr. Lomux was way too mean. But I liked playing sports with Mookie, since he didn't care whether he won or not. He just loved to play.

In language arts, we read about Edgar Allan Poe. By the end of the lesson, I actually felt my own life was sort of normal. In art, we got to do whatever we wanted, so I drew space aliens with giant heads and tiny arms. Then I drew more aliens with giant arms and tiny heads. But at least the aliens were the only weird thing I ran into during the afternoon.

"Want to play ball with us?" I asked Abigail after school.

She scrunched up her nose. "As thrilling as that sounds, I think I'd rather check out what's left of that spybot." She pointed to the bits of metal squirrel scattered near the curb. "There could be clues to its origin."

Mookie and I didn't see any more suspicious bushes or squirrels on the way home. It looked like I could relax. I grabbed my ball from the garage and we went down the street to the little park two blocks from my house. It's really just a field, without any playground equipment or other stuff—not even any basketball hoops—but a field was all we needed.

We had the place pretty much to ourselves. A couple kids were kicking a soccer ball around at the other end. A woman with curly white hair was sitting in a car across the street, reading a newspaper. Maybe she was waiting for the kids.

I flicked the ball to Mookie.

"Oops!" It slipped out of his hands. He chased after it, dove on it, then raised it in the air and shouted, "Fumble recovered by Mookie Vetch! Yaaayyyyyy!" He did a victory dance, fell down, got up, then turned toward me and yelled, "Go long!"

I ran down the field. That was another thing I liked. Before I'd gotten splashed with Hurt-Be-Gone, I'd had asthma, so I tried not to run. Now, I could run all day without losing my breath. You can't lose what you don't have.

"I'm open!" I shouted.

"Five seconds on the clock! Four! Three!" Mookie hurled the ball. He actually had a pretty good arm. Lots of strength. No control. The ball spiraled over my head. I sprinted, reached up, and tried to catch it. The ball hit my right index finger.

The ball kept going.

So did my finger.

"Shoot." This wasn't good. I looked around for my finger. It had landed ten feet away from me, near a clump of dandelions.

"Do the crawly thing," Mookie said as he jogged over to me.

"Not now," I said. "Abigail told me to be careful. Remember?"

"Oh, come on, nobody's watching. It's so cool. Pleeeeeease."

"Okay." I guess there was no reason not to. And he was right—it was sort of cool.

I flexed my finger. Even though it wasn't attached to my body, it curled. I made it crawl across the grass toward me like an inchworm. When it reached my feet, I picked it up and pulled out the glue bottle I always carried. As I twisted the cap open, I laughed.

"What's so funny?" Mookie asked. "I mean, beside seeing your finger fly through the air?"

I held up the glue bottle. "I used to carry my inhaler wherever I went. I was afraid to leave the house without it. Now that I finally got rid of it, I have to carry this."

Mookie laughed, too. "I never thought I'd be friends with someone who was so stuck up."

"Or stuck together." I smeared some of the mixture on the broken end of my finger. Mookie stepped back and clamped his hands over his ears, since he knew what was coming.

"Ahhhgggggg!" Even though I was expecting it, the pain from the nerves knitting back together was enough to make me howl like a coyote.

The soccer players stared at us from across the field. Mookie looked back at them and howled. He dropped on

37

all fours, ran around like an animal, and pretended to bite at my ankles. The soccer players shrugged and went back to their game.

By then, the pain had faded. I didn't want to think what it would be like if—or when—I broke something bigger than a finger. But I knew I'd have to face that sooner or later. I just hoped I didn't lose my head. I couldn't imagine looking up at my body from a head that was rolling across the ground.

"You want to quit?" Mookie asked.

"Yeah. The glue needs to set. Hey, what's that noise?"

"I don't hear anything," Mookie said.

"Something's buzzing. I think it's coming from that car." As I turned, I saw a flash of light. The woman in the parked car was watching us with binoculars.

Without thinking, I ran toward the car. Before I got there, she peeled out, swerving away from the curb and flying down the street. Something tumbled from the window as the car disappeared around a curve.

"She's a he," I said, pointing to the wig that had fallen to the street.

"Wow, he took off fast," Mookie said. "Maybe he had to go to the bathroom."

I shook my head. "I think I'm the one whose life is about to end up in the toilet."

Mookie and I both jumped as we heard a crash like someone ramming into a hundred metal garbage cans.

"Let's go!" We ran down the street. When we got past

the curve in the road, I saw that the car had smashed against a telephone pole.

"I hope nobody's hurt," Mookie said.

We raced to the car. Part of me didn't want to get too close. I really didn't want to see someone who'd been smashed up.

I slowed down enough that Mookie got there ahead of me. "She's not a he," he said.

I stared through the driver's window. "She's an *it*."

The driver wasn't a person. It was some sort of mechanical dummy. The flash of light I'd seen hadn't been from binoculars—it had been from electronic eyes. They looked like the zoom lenses on a camera. There was a bunch of equipment in the backseat, including something with an antenna.

"How did it drive?" Mookie asked.

"Badly," I said. There weren't any other cars around. Whoever was doing the driving was doing it from somewhere else. So they'd seen everything. "It must be remote controlled."

A couple sparks shot from the thing's head.

"Let's go," I said.

"Just a second," Mookie said. "I want to check out the stuff in the backseat."

Smoke drifted from the robot's ears. Its face started to melt. I remembered what had happened to the squirrel.

I grabbed Mookie's arm and yanked hard. "Run!"

We were less than a half block away when the thing

inside the car exploded, blowing the doors off the car. A moment later, the car exploded, too. But I'd saved us. I couldn't help imagining the applause of a crowd of spectators. I could almost hear their conversations.

Who is that amazing zombie hero?

So dead, and yet so brave.

I want to be like him when I die.

"What next?" Mookie asked as we jogged away. "Helicopters? Flying saucers? Guys with jet packs?"

"I wish I knew."

Mookie looked back over his shoulder. "I never thought hanging out with a dead guy could get you killed."

6

Model Behavior

When I got home, I headed for the computer. I really wanted to see if I could find out who would have that much electronic spy stuff. But I remembered what Abigail had said. *Don't go online.* The last time I'd ignored her advice, back at the field, it had caused trouble. This time, I was going to listen to her. I left the computer alone.

It was just me and Mom for dinner, since Dad had to work late. Mookie's folks were back from their trip, so he didn't stay over. That was okay. He's my best friend, and I like hanging around with him, but when he's asleep, he makes all sorts of noises. From both ends. It's sort of like having a barnyard in your bedroom. Or a tuba convention.

I got under the covers and closed my eyes. Every once in a while, I still tried to sleep. It never worked. I didn't need covers, either. I don't ever feel hot or cold. But habits are hard to drop. And there's something nice about being under a pile of blankets.

I got out of bed, reached behind my bookcase, and pulled out my sketchbook. It was all there—my whole superhero plan. I was still trying to come up with the perfect name for myself. Zombie Guy. Zomboy. Mr. Undead. Captain Corpse. None of those seemed right. But I had the costume figured out. It would be black, with a big Z on the front, made out of three bones.

Mookie would need a costume, too, since he'd be my sidekick. He'd need a name, too. I was sort of thinking it would be "The Stumbler."

Abigail could make me all sorts of cool stuff, like Batman had. I could slink through the shadows of East Craven, looking for people to save. It would be perfect and awesome. Best of all, it really could happen—unless the guy who was spying on me messed everything up.

After a while, I put the sketchbook away and dug through my closet. At the bottom of a box of old toys, I found a half-finished model of an Indy race car—the kind with the big spoiler. I dumped the parts on my desk and unfolded the instructions. I took my time putting the model together, but I was still finished way before morning.

I got back in bed. Around me, the house creaked and groaned. Outside, I could hear cars going past. I could swear I could almost hear them all the way across town. After a long wait, the sun rose. I heard someone in the kitchen. I waited a while longer, then got out of bed and put on my school clothes. I was at the kitchen table before Mom came downstairs.

She ruffled my hair. "Well, you're up with the chickens. Did you get enough sleep?"

"Sure. I got as much as I needed." I noticed there was a half-empty coffee cup in the sink already. "Dad left?"

"He had to go in early again. He's finishing up an important project." She walked over to the fridge. "How about a nice, big breakfast?"

"I'm okay with cereal." It was one of the easier things to pretend to eat. Especially puffed cereal. I could push it around in my bowl, smush it down, and then dump the whole mess in the garbage without my parents getting suspicious.

Before I left, I peeked out the front window. As far as I could tell, everything was normal. All the way to school, I kept trying to spot someone following me. But the street was quiet. None of the people driving by even looked at me. I didn't see the same car more than once. There were no squirrels with cameras. There weren't even any suspicious-looking plants.

"Any sign of that guy?" Mookie asked when I got to school.

"Nope."

"That's good. Maybe he lost interest in you."

"Lost interest?" I thought back to our game of catch

in the park. "I'm pretty sure whoever was controlling that car saw me make my finger crawl across the field."

"Then maybe you scared him off," Mookie said.

"That would be nice, but I don't think it'll be that easy."

Mookie started to laugh. "Hey—you made me think of a joke. How can you tell that zombies like music?"

"I don't know. How?"

He snapped both thumbs, then looked around like he'd dropped something. "They're always snapping their fingers!" He collapsed to the ground, shaking with laughter.

There was no way I'd admit it, but I guess it was sort of funny.

Abigail had a different theory about why nobody was following me. "I think he saw what he needed to see. Now he's planning his next move. Or maybe he's analyzing whatever he saw. It's not every day you deal with a zombie."

"So you think I'll see that guy again?" I asked. "Or one of his robot thingies?"

"Probably. But it works both ways. The more of them we see, the better chance we have of figuring out what's going on. I already have a clue or two. The battery in the squirrel is from Australia. But the body seems to be made from American steel."

"What does that mean?" I asked.

"I have no idea yet," Abigail said.

That didn't make me feel any better. I tried not to think about it as we headed toward class.

That night, I finished the other three half-done models in my closet. Now, I had two race cars, a jet plane, a rocket ship, and nothing to do.

Maybe I really did scare him off, I thought as I walked to school Wednesday morning.

"I need a hobby," I told Mookie. "I have way too much time to kill after my parents go to bed."

"You could collect butterflies," he said.

"That's sort of hard to do at night."

"So collect moths. They're cooler, anyhow." He squeezed his fingers into a fist. "Especially the ones with the fat, squishy bodies."

I didn't ask Abigail's advice. I figured she'd tell me to do something way too complicated, like build my own nuclear reactor or raise striped rabbits.

There was a weird silence mixed in with all the noise at lunch. We were halfway through the period before I realized what was missing. "You aren't making any jokes," I said to Denali. "You didn't even make a joke about when we learned about pi in math class this morning."

She answered me with a small shrug.

"What's wrong?" Abigail asked.

Denali opened her mouth, closed it, sniffed, sobbed, then finally said, "We might have to move."

"Why?" we all asked.

"My folks' shop isn't doing too good," Denali said. "Everyone is going to the new dry cleaner in Hurston Lakes. If business doesn't get better, Dad says we'll have to move to Florida and stay with my grandparents."

"Things will get better," I said. I couldn't imagine our lunch table, or my classes, without Denali.

The other kids all said encouraging things. Except for Abigail, who seemed to be thinking deep thoughts. By the end of lunch, Denali looked a little less sad. I guess it helps to know that people care what happens to you.

Let's get you paired up," Mr. Lomux said at the start of gym class. He began calling names. Rodney got matched with Omar Wilkes, who's big but not very strong. I watched Omar's face when he heard the news. He looked like he was trying to swallow a fistful of sand.

Mookie ended up with Dilby, and I was matched with Ferdinand. We lined up on the mat, face-to-face with our partners. I noticed Ferdinand was trembling.

"What's wrong?" I asked him.

"You're going to hurt me," he said.

I almost laughed, but I could see he was totally serious. "How am I going to hurt you?"

"You could break my neck," Ferdinand said. "Lots of

wrestlers get their necks broke. Or you could rupture my liver. There's tons of ways you could hurt me. I'm fragile."

I glanced at Mr. Lomux to make sure he wasn't paying any attention to us, then leaned toward Ferdinand and whispered, "Look—I don't like this any more than you do. Let's cooperate and we won't get hurt. Okay?"

"Cooperate?"

"Yeah. We'll make it look like we're fighting hard. But we'll take turns getting pinned and stuff."

Ferdinand nodded. "Good idea. But just don't hurt me. Okay?"

"Let's see what you got," Mr. Lomux said. "One pair at a time. Let's go."

When our turn came, Ferdinand and I pretended to struggle. He grabbed my legs. I grunted and leaned toward him for a second, like I was fighting hard, then flopped back. I made sure to fall softly, since I didn't want to snap anything. We kept at it until Mr. Lomux blew his whistle.

"I didn't break my neck," Ferdinand whispered as we got up. "That's great."

"I know the feeling." I watched the rest of the kids. When it was Rodney's turn, he dove toward Omar, wrapped his arms around Omar's legs, lifted him up, and slammed him down on his back, driving his shoulder into Omar's stomach.

Omar produced a sound I didn't think a human could make. It was sort of like what you'd get if you crossed a bagpipe with a goose and a bassoon.

"Signature move!" Rodney shouted.

I figured Mr. Lomux would yell at Rodney for being too rough, but he just smiled and said, "Good start." Then he showed us a takedown and told us to practice it with our partner.

That was even easier to fake. As Ferdinand and I were going through the moves, I noticed every kid around me suddenly grab his nose and make gagging sounds. I grabbed my own nose and pretended I was suffering.

The whole class looked over at Mookie.

"Hey—I didn't do it," he said.

Everyone kept staring.

"What? Really—it's not me." He sniffed the air. "That's not mine. No way. I had hot dogs last night." He sniffed again. "Definitely not a hot dog fart. That smells like a broccoli fart. Or brussels sprouts. They're pretty hard to tell apart."

"All of you—knock it off!" Mr. Lomux screamed. "Don't be such big babies. Real men can handle anything. We don't go crying about a little bit of gas. It's time to get tough. I know just how to do it."

I didn't like the sound of that, the look in his eyes, or the scary smile on his face.

7

A Sock in the face

"Take off your socks," Mr. Lomux shouted.

"Our socks?" Mookie said.

"You heard me." Six veins bulged in Mr. Lomux's forehead.

We slipped out of our sneakers and took off our socks.

"Hold them against your nose," he said.

We all stared at each other. Mr. Lomux repeated the command, at full volume, with the help of seven veins.

We smelled our socks.

I didn't mind, since I didn't actually have to breathe in. But I could tell it was pretty hard on the rest of the kids. I saw bodies jerking as kids gagged. Mookie dropped to his knees. Then he flopped on his side and started shaking.

I was about to run for help when I realized he was joking.

Mr. Lomux didn't even look at Mookie. "This will make real men out of you."

He had us spend the last five minutes of class breathing through our socks.

"Man, I wish they'd transferred him," Mookie said when we were leaving the gym.

"It's your fault they didn't," Adam said to me.

He was right. Mr. Lomux would probably have been transferred to Borloff Lower Elementary if we'd lost the field day competition against Perrin Hall Academy. Before that, our school had lost six years in a row. But thanks to my zombie skills, I'd won the day for us and made Mr. Lomux look good.

"Yeah," Mookie said. "I heard the new gym teacher at Borloff is awesome. I'll bet he'd love to come here."

"And Mr. Lomux has gotten even worse since we won," Adam said. "He's trying to turn us into some sort of superkids. I think he's like a tiger that suddenly got a taste of human flesh. Now he wants more."

"Yeah," I said. "Except he's like a loser who suddenly got a taste of victory."

"All I can tell you is, I'm wearing clean socks from now on," Mookie said. "If I'd known they smelled that bad after just three days, I would have changed them sooner."

"You should be happy it wasn't your underwear," Adam said.

Mookie nodded. "That would be a death sentence."

"And I should never eat broccoli again," Adam said.

I saw another squirrel on the way home. But this one was flesh and blood. And not very bright. It ran right into the side of a tree. At least it didn't explode in a shower of metal parts.

"I made your favorite," Mom said at dinner. She plopped a stuffed cabbage onto my plate.

"Thanks. It looks great." I couldn't even guess how or when she got the idea that I loved stuffed cabbage. But at least, like most stuffed things, it was easy to make it look like I'd eaten some.

Dad had work spread out at the table. "Big project?" I asked him.

He nodded. "It's a killer."

"You really should take a break while you eat," Mom said.

Dad nodded and pushed the papers aside. He looked tired. I figured, unlike me, he'd have no problem sleeping.

That night, I sat in bed, wondering whether it was safe to go online. Abigail said the guy was probably off analyzing what he'd seen. Actually, right now, he was probably asleep in bed, like everyone except me.

I searched through my closet for something to do. I

didn't find anything, unless I wanted to try to beat myself at checkers or Battleship.

I really needed to use the computer. I'd been playing this huge multiplayer game, *Vampyre Stalker*, for a couple weeks now. I'd advanced my character up to level 42, and was just about to enter the crypt of Nastydamus, a level 48 vampire. I'd saved all the money I'd earned in the game and bought a hollow silver cross that was filled with a superconcentrated mixture of garlic and holy water. I was dying to try it out. I was pretty sure it would turn Nastydamus into a pile of steaming ashes.

Was it safe to log on?

Mookie's dad might think people watched everything you did on a computer, but he also swore that the moon landing was a fake. And he'd told Mookie he couldn't have a cell phone, because the signals from them attracted wild animals. I think he might have made that up to save money.

I tiptoed downstairs and went to the computer. In the game, I was Staker Slaymaster, a fifth-generation vampire hunter with awesome bladed-weapon fighting skills and some basic spell-casting ability. The last time I'd played, I'd reached the edge of the Village of Mobrule, which had been wiped out by Nastydamus. A gravel path led up a hillside to the crypt.

I wasn't online for more than thirty seconds when a peasant walked toward me. A message popped up in my status window.

Peter Plowshare: *I know who you are.*

My hand froze on the mouse. Answer or ignore? It didn't have to be the guy who was spying on me. Maybe it was just some player who was trying to be mysterious. I waited to see if he'd leave.

Peter Plowshare: *We need to meet.*

I didn't like this. But I couldn't walk away. I typed a message and clicked the SEND icon.

Staker Slaymaster: *I'm just a kid. Leave me alone.*

Peter Plowshare: *You were a kid. You're more now.*

I typed: *That's not true.* Then I deleted it. It was pointless to try to tell him he was wrong. But I wanted to find out why he was stalking me.

Staker Slaymaster: *What do you want?*

Peter Plowshare: *To talk with you, face-to-face.*

Staker Slaymaster: *Then why are you talking to me online?*

Peter Plowshare: *I didn't want to scare you off. But I need to see you.*

Staker Slaymaster: *I don't need to see you.*

Peter Plowshare: *I'll be in touch. Look for me. Don't be afraid.*

The peasant walked away. I sat there with my dead fingers draped across the mouse. The game didn't seem very important right now. There was another game going on, outside the computer. A real-life one. Or maybe real-death.

Let's Call It a Meeting

Once again, I was at the breakfast table early.

"You're really being a responsible student," Mom said. "I haven't had to wake you at all this week. You used to be such a little sleepyhead. But not anymore."

"Thanks." It felt weird getting credit for something I didn't have any control over. But there was one thing I could sort of control, if only for a little while. I didn't want to deal with anyone this morning—especially not someone who could build mechanical spy squirrels and hack into computer systems. "I've got a lot of stuff to carry. Can I get a ride?" I didn't explain that I was carrying most of it in my mind, and not my backpack.

I reached school way ahead of everyone. When Mookie showed up, I told him what happened.

"You should've hit him with your sword and made him tell you everything," Mookie said.

"I'll try to remember that for next time," I said.

By then, Abigail had joined us. I filled her in about my conversation with the peasant in the *Vampyre Stalker* game. "I wish I knew something about him. Anything at all."

"We know a lot," Abigail said. "For example, he claims he doesn't want to scare you off. That means he needs your cooperation. Whatever he's after, he can't just take it."

"I guess that's good." I liked the idea that I had something so special that someone would go through all kinds of effort to get it.

"I'm also pretty sure this guy has a lot of resources," Abigail said. "The squirrel was more advanced than anything I've seen or heard about. This isn't someone playing spy games for fun. He's serious."

"So, do you think I should talk to him when he shows up?"

"Absolutely," Abigail said. "You have to find out what he knows, and what he wants. But let him do all the talking. Just listen and nod as much as you can. That's the best way to learn what's going on."

I invited Mookie and Abigail to my place after school. The first thing Abigail did when she got inside was head for the kitchen.

"I'm going to take care of death row," she said.

She filled Mom's watering can and took it to the family room to rescue the plants Mom always forgot about.

"You're only delaying their death," I said.

"You're only delaying your meeting," she said.

"What are you talking about?"

"You're using Mookie and me to avoid facing this guy. That's fine. I'm glad we're hanging out. I've become quite fond of socializing. But you're going to have to deal with him."

"I know." I was still getting used to one huge change in my life. I wasn't ready for another. "I guess I just wanted a little more time."

Abigail drained the last of the water into a pot on the shelf. "We all do."

I looked at her, and then looked away. I knew what she meant, but I didn't know what to say. Her dad had died last year. I'm sure she'd have given anything to have more time with him. I reached for the watering can. "Here. I'll get some more."

My time ran out Friday morning on the way to school. Two blocks from home, I heard footsteps behind me. I knew who I'd see even before I turned around.

"Hello, young man," he said. He was wearing normal clothes this time, like someone who worked in an office. I noticed he was holding an onion bagel.

"You aren't hiding in a bush," I said.

"There's no reason to hide. We've learned enough about you to know we need to talk. Do you have any idea how special you are?"

I started to answer him, then remembered what Abigail had told me. *Don't talk. Listen.* I shrugged.

"There's something special about you. Very special."

I realized he didn't know everything. He hadn't mentioned anything specific. And he'd said, *We've learned enough.* So he wasn't working alone. Though I guess that wasn't a big surprise, since he seemed to have all sorts of equipment.

"You must be proud of what you can do," he said. "Really and truly proud of all your special abilities."

It was obvious he was trying to get me to talk. There was no way I was opening my mouth. I just stared at him. After a moment, he gave me a small nod, as if to let me know I'd won the first round. I got the feeling he hadn't been trying too hard.

"I'm impressed. You seem to have a gift for the kind of work we do. Take this cell phone." He held out the bagel.

"It looks like a bagel," I said.

"That's the beauty of it. Give it a twist."

"Will it explode?"

"Now you're being tedious. Just take it."

I took the bagel from him and twisted it. It slid open, revealing a screen and touch pad. "Why would you want a phone that looked like a bagel?"

He smiled. "I can think of a million reasons. But

never mind that. Listen—my number is programmed under 'Mr. Peter Murphy.' You need our support. Call me when you're ready to discuss your future."

"Don't hold your breath."

He started to walk away. Then he turned back. "Oh, by the way, there are some serious side effects from exposure to the corpse flower. But I suspect you're already aware of that."

Twitch Craft

My jaw dropped when he mentioned the corpse flower. That was the ingredient Abigail's Uncle Zardo had used by mistake in the Hurt-Be-Gone formula. I looked at the phone for a while, half afraid it would explode. Finally, I shoved it in my pocket and headed to school.

My conversation with Mr. Murphy took long enough that Mookie and Abigail were already out front when I got to school. I explained what happened and showed them the phone.

"Toss it," Mookie said. "You definitely need to toss it."

"Call him," Abigail said.

"Ahhhgggg!" Mookie wailed. "How come I always guess wrong? That does it. I'm letting everyone else go before me from now on. Especially you, Abigail."

"Why do you think I should call?" I asked Abigail.

"You've gone this far. You talked to him. It's obvious he knows something. Maybe he's not a bad guy. He took his time approaching you so you wouldn't get scared. He didn't hurt you. He even said he might be able to help you."

"A bit of help would be nice." I realized he could have dragged me into a van if he wanted to kidnap me. My new abilities didn't include super strength. Though I guess if he'd grabbed my arm, I could escape by breaking it off.

"Call him after school," Abigail said.

"Yeah. Or maybe I'll wait until tonight. Or tomorrow morning. But it will be the weekend by then. Monday might be better."

"Nathan, stop stalling," Abigail said. "You need to get this settled. Call him right after school. If he wants to meet you somewhere, Mookie and I will follow you."

"I'm a great follower," Mookie said. He took a couple steps on tiptoe, then stumbled off the curb.

"Okay. I'll do it." I liked the idea that they'd know where I was going.

Abigail flashed me a grin. "And we won't need a junky old paper-towel-tube telescope. I'll call Mom and ask her to bring me my binoculars." Then her grin faded. "Oh, phooey. I can't. They're gone."

"We'll be fine without them," I told her. She'd lost all her stuff last month in a fire. I guess she'd had some cool equipment for her science experiments. Now, it was ashes.

Abigail seemed sad during social studies, but her smile returned when we got to science class and she spotted the frog on Ms. Delambre's desk.

I walked over and stared at it. It was either deeply asleep or dead.

"Looks like one of your relatives," Mookie said.

"Shut up." I stared at the frog. It wasn't moving at all. Definitely dead.

"He croaked," Denali said from the table next to ours.

I was glad she was getting her sense of humor back, even if that was sort of an old joke.

"Galvani," Abigail whispered. Her eyes sparkled like this was a magic word.

I looked at her. "What?"

She smiled. "That's probably the lesson. I think you'll find it interesting."

Ms. Delambre came in, and we all took our seats.

"Luigi Galvani was an Italian physician," Ms. Delambre said.

I glanced at Abigail. She gave me an *I told you so* shrug. As much as she felt she needed to hide her brains from her classmates, I realized she enjoyed sharing her secret with Mookie and me. I nodded toward her and clapped my hands quietly.

Up front, Ms. Delambre explained about Galvani's

experiment, and how he'd discovered that he could make a frog move when he applied electricity to its muscles.

"We'll have to try that with you sometime," Abigail whispered.

"Nobody's experimenting on me," I said.

Maybe that was true for the next hour or two, but Mr. Lomux's class also seemed sort of like a science experiment. When we got to the gym, there were buckets lined up against one wall.

"Now what?" Adam asked.

"Maybe he expects everyone to throw up," Mookie said.

"It's going to be something a lot less pleasant than that," I said.

"Line up over here," Mr. Lomux shouted, pointing to the buckets.

I found a spot by a bucket. It was filled with water and chunks of ice.

"Put your hands in," Mr. Lomux said.

I stooped down and put my hands in the water. It didn't bother me. But I heard yelps and gasps all around. I remembered what it felt like the last time I got into a snowball fight without gloves. It's no fun having frozen fingers.

"First person to take his hands out runs twenty laps," Mr. Lomux said.

"I'm dying," Mookie said. "I'd rather run."

"Hang on," I told him. "Someone will drop out soon enough."

"I'm afraid of frostbite." Ferdinand pulled his hands out. "I don't want to lose a finger."

"Next one, twenty push-ups," Mr. Lomux said.

That was Dilby, who jammed his hands under his armpits.

Pretty soon, there were just five of us left. Then it was down to two—me and Rodney. I could tell he was hurting. His arms were shaking and his lips were blue. I didn't care about winning. But I cared about stopping him from winning. So I kept my hands in the water until he gave up.

As we were lugging our buckets into the locker room to dump them, Rodney bumped me and said, "You're lucky you're too skinny to wrestle me. I'd kill you."

I stared right back at him. "No, you wouldn't." I could almost see myself in a superhero mask and costume, saving someone from Rodney.

"You're gonna get it, Abercrombie. Sooner or later, I'll get my chance. And it will be worth waiting for."

Keep dreaming.

Before I could say it, Mr. Lomux shouted at us to get moving. "Pair up. I want to see your takedowns. One at a time."

As I watched one perfect takedown after another, I realized that a lot of the kids had decided to fake it. They worked together, so the kid shooting the move looked great. Rodney wasn't playing along, of course. He seemed to like flattening Omar, and not letting Omar pull off any moves on him.

"Excellent!" Mr. Lomux yelled after both sides took a turn. "Let's do it again."

We repeated the drill. By now, Mr. Lomux was almost glowing. There wasn't a vein in sight. I could swear his head might even have gotten a bit smaller. "Great! Wonderful! I've never seen so many wrestlers with so much potential."

I guess he was too thrilled by our attacks to stop and wonder why nobody had any defensive skills. That didn't matter. As long as it kept him happy and kept us from getting hurt, it was a perfect system.

On the way out of the gym, a couple kids patted me on the back and said, "Great idea, Nate."

"You're a hero," Ferdinand said.

"A real genius," Adam said.

Dilby pulled his hand out from under his shirt, where he'd been scratching his belly, and held it up for a high five. I flashed him a thumbs-up and raced away.

"I think we're going to get through this whole wrestling thing in one piece," Mookie said.

"I think so." But I had something else to get through. And it might be a lot tougher than gym class.

After school, I met up with Mookie and Abigail at the seesaws.

"Here goes," I said.

"You'll be fine," Abigail said.

I pulled out the bagel, gave it a twist, and called Mr. Murphy. He answered on the second ring.

"Yes?"

"Let's meet," I said.

10

▼

Grout and About

Go to Decarlo Street and get on the Number Six bus. I'll call again with more instructions."

"He wants me to take the Number Six bus," I told Abigail and Mookie.

"Cool," Mookie said. "This is like a spy movie."

We walked to Decarlo Street and got on the bus. A couple minutes later, music spilled from my pocket. "Stars and Stripes Forever." Just like the high school marching band played. People near me turned to glare. I pulled out the bagel phone and answered it.

"Get off at Bleek Street," he said.

I got off. So did Mookie and Abigail. The bagel rang

again. "Take the crosstown bus. But tell your friends not to follow you."

The line went dead.

"You're not supposed to follow me," I said.

Mookie spun around like he was tracking the zigzag flight of a supersonic hornet. "This is creepy. Where are they? How did he know we're with you? They must be watching you."

"I don't think so," Abigail said. "I think he said it just in case Nathan brought friends. Let's keep following him. If they can really see us, they'll tell him again."

It's a good thing we had bus passes. Mr. Murphy had me ride around town for almost an hour. But he didn't say anything else about my friends. I realized, as smart as he might be, Abigail was smarter. That made me feel better. Finally, he told me to get off at Lurch Street, which was only three blocks from where I'd started. There were some small office buildings on the street, and a store or two. The phone rang as soon as I stepped off the bus.

"There's a museum in the middle of the block," he said. "Go inside."

Museum? I didn't know there was a museum in town. I told Abigail and Mookie what was happening.

"We'll wait around the corner at the Gas 'n' Snack," Abigail said, "just in case they're watching the entrance."

I headed down the street. Sure enough, right in the middle of the block, I found an old brick building with chipped white windowsills and crumbly front steps. It was like the building version of a zombie. Faded black letters on the door read: THE NATIONAL MUSEUM OF TILE AND GROUT.

Tile and grout? No wonder I'd never heard of it. I totally wasn't interested in tiles, and I wasn't even sure what grout was. I tried the door, even though it looked like the place was locked up.

It opened.

The inside was a lot nicer than the outside. It reminded me of a really large version of the principal's office, without the New York Giants posters. The walls were painted light green, and the furniture seemed pretty new. There was an old woman behind a desk, knitting an orange scarf.

"I'm sorry," I said. "I think I'm in the wrong place."

She looked up from her knitting. "Are you here to see the tile collection?"

"No."

"Are you interested in our special grout display?"

"Definitely not."

"How about the hall of trowels?"

"No way."

"Kilns?"

"Uh-uh."

"The history of clay?"

"Not a chance."

"Then you're in the right place." She put down the needles and pointed to an elevator in the middle of the rear wall. As I walked over, the doors slid open.

I stepped inside. *Is this a mistake?*

I had no way to answer that question. The doors closed. There was a seat against the back wall—the kind you see on a roller coaster.

"Please have a seat."

The recorded voice came from a speaker in the ceiling. It sounded friendly, like my aunt Nina. I sat.

The bar dropped down over my head, cushioning my chest.

"Please remove any loose items."

I didn't have any loose items, except maybe my fingers and toes.

"Please hold on."

I gripped the handles.

The elevator car rotated a quarter turn. Something in the walls hummed like a jet engine warming up.

"Yiiiikes!"

I was thrust hard against the back of the seat as the car shot forward. The acceleration grew until I was pinned flat. I had no idea how fast I was moving, but I was pretty sure I'd never gone this fast before in an elevator. Or even a train. After a couple minutes, the car suddenly swung around the other way.

"Whooaaaa!" I shouted like I was on a carnival ride. It was actually pretty awesome. I felt more pressure as I hurtled backwards. I guess the car was slowing down as quickly as it had sped up.

The car coasted to a stop. It rotated again, and the door opened. As I stepped out, I noticed there was a whole row of elevator doors on either side of me. Each had a number on it. Mine was thirteen.

Mr. Murphy was waiting for me. Once again, he was dressed pretty normally, in a dark suit, white shirt, and red tie. "Hello, Nathan. Thank you for coming."

I couldn't remember whether I'd ever told him my name. I guess it didn't matter. Anyone who wanted to learn my name would be able to find it out pretty easily. I handed him the bagel phone. "What was all of that stuff with the buses?"

"We had to make sure you weren't being followed."

I was going to ask who would possibly want to follow me, but I realized I was face-to-face with at least one person who fit that description. So I guess there could be others. I also realized he'd done a terrible job of making sure I wasn't followed.

"How'd you know my friends were with me?"

"I didn't." He flashed me a smug smile. "Until now."

I managed to keep from returning the smile. That was easy enough—dead kids only smile when they want to. I guess he was trying to show me how clever he was. I decided not to let him know that I—or at least Abigail—was pretty clever, too. Probably more clever than he was. Even if she didn't have a cool elevator that moved as fast as a rocket ship. Or robot squirrels.

"Why did you bring me here?" I asked.

"I'm a recruiter for BUM."

"You're recruiting bums? Are you calling me names?"

"Be You Em," he said, spelling the name. "The Bureau of Useful Misadventures." He spoke the words as if they were the name of someone he loved. "As far as I can tell, you've certainly had a whopper of a misadventure. Something drastic has happened to you."

I was about to tell him he was wrong when he held up his hand to stop me. He turned and walked down a hallway. I followed him.

"Where are we?" I didn't even know if I was still in New Jersey. The elevator had gone so fast, I figured I could be in New York, Pennsylvania, or Delaware. Maybe even Maryland.

"That's a secret." He leaned over until his mouth was right next to my ear and whispered, "If you haven't figured it out already, this is not exactly a public organization."

He stepped into a room on his left. There was a huge flat-panel screen on one wall, even bigger than the TV Adam's parents had. He picked up a remote control and pressed a button.

I saw myself on the field with Mookie, right after I'd missed the football. The camera zoomed to a shot of my index finger as I made it crawl back to me. The video showed me gluing the finger on, and only ended when I'd caught sight of the car and started to run across the field. Then it looped back to the beginning.

"Very impressive," Mr. Murphy said. "But also very dangerous for you. I suspect this isn't the first bone you've broken, is it?"

"No." I didn't see any reason to lie about that. "I've snapped a couple."

71

"But I also suspect you have some very interesting abilities, beyond your control of severed parts. Is that correct?"

"I guess."

"Don't be modest, Nathan," Mr. Murphy said. "We need to know. As I said, this is the Bureau of *Useful* Misadventures. We don't care if you can tell M-and-M's apart by taste or play the saxophone with your nose. We want to know if you can fly through the air or melt steel with your eyes."

"I can do some stuff," I admitted. "But I still don't know what you want."

Mr. Murphy pointed to a leather couch on the wall opposite the TV. "Have a seat, lad. I have a story to tell you."

Strengthening the Offer

I sat. *He* pushed another button on the remote, then slipped into an easy chair that faced the couch. An old black-and-white photograph appeared on the screen, showing a kid who was maybe twelve or thirteen.

"In 1915, in a village near London, a boy just a little older than you was playing with fireworks. When he saw his mother coming, he panicked and shoved a large lit firecracker under his sweater. He blew a hole in his stomach. He lived, but he was left with a flap of skin covering this hole."

"That's pretty gross," I said.

"And pretty useful. British troops used him to smuggle documents across enemy lines during the First World War. Nobody suspected a young boy. And even when the enemy searched him, the documents were safe. It's highly unlikely anyone would give the scarred tissue of his stomach a close examination."

"I guess that's kind of cool." I imagined what it would be like to be a spy, doing special work for my government.

"In 1943, in Appleton, Wisconsin, a teenager who was trying to fix a broken toaster jolted herself with enough electricity to melt her fillings. From that point on, she was able to intercept certain radio frequencies in her head. More important, and much harder to explain, her brain was able to unscramble coded messages. She proved to be very helpful in the war effort."

"Kids are always messing around with stuff. I tried to take our toaster apart once."

"Exactly." Mr. Murphy nodded. "Young people have an endless capacity for experimenting with things that are better left alone. Often, the results are tragic. Rarely, one of these misadventures produces amazing results. As in your case."

"But who are you?" I asked.

"I told you. We're BUM."

"I mean, are you with the government?"

"We're independent. We were formed many years ago by an extraordinarily wealthy man who had done some bad things and wanted to make up for them. We serve many governments," he said. "BUM provides assistance to the United States, Great Britain, Canada, Australia, and other allied democratic nations. We're here to help the free world."

That was good to hear. It sounded like Mr. Murphy was with the good guys. "What sort of things do you do?"

"Whatever needs doing," he said.

"What's with all the robots and stuff?" I asked.

"As I said, we have a huge supply of funds at our disposal. Potential agents like you come along rarely. We need to do something with our time and money while we search for candidates."

"How'd you find me?"

"We have lots of ways to search for misadventures. For example, there are certain people who are much more likely to inspire an accident than the average citizen. We keep an eye on those people."

"So you were watching—" I was about to say *Abigail's uncle*. But I caught myself. I didn't want to give Mr. Murphy any information, even if it was stuff he probably already knew.

He nodded. "Yes, we were keeping an eye on Zardo Goldberg. And we learned of his efforts to obtain the corpse flower. We knew it had highly promising properties, though we didn't know the details. After we learned of his arrest, one of our agents went to the lab and saw the spill. He took a sample, which we analyzed. We're still not sure about everything that could happen, but we suspected anyone exposed to this formula might suffer insomnia, among other things. I assume you aren't sleeping."

I shrugged and waited for him to continue.

"Along with various other methods of investigation, we began checking homes within twenty miles of the lab for online activity at night, especially in accounts where there hadn't been any such activity previously. Your account popped right up. After that, I merely needed to see whether you were more than just a normal boy who had trouble sleeping."

"So you were spying on me?" I didn't like that idea.

"Well, we *are* spies. So, yes—we were spying on you. And we tracked your Internet usage. And, if I had to, I could listen to your phone calls, read your mail, and access your school records. But I don't need to know those things. I want to learn about your abilities. What can you do? What use is your misadventure? But before we talk any further, I want to show you a good reason to cooperate with us."

He got up from the chair and headed out the door. I couldn't even guess what he was planning to show me. I was still pretty amazed by the fact that I'd taken a high-speed trip through a tunnel to a secret organization. At this point, nothing would surprise me.

We walked down the hall to a place that looked like a doctor's examination room. There was a large table in the center of the floor, with some kind of machine above it. There was also a woman wearing a white lab coat. I wasn't sure I liked that. The last time I'd been near a person in a lab coat, I'd been drenched with Hurt-Be-Gone and turned into a zombie.

"We haven't had much time to investigate all the effects of the corpse flower. But we're pretty sure your bones are growing brittle," Mr. Murphy said. "We can fix that. Let me give you a small demonstration. Put your hand in here." He placed a large plastic container in the middle of the table.

The machine had all kinds of wires attached to it. I had the feeling it had been put together pretty quickly. "It won't explode, will it?"

"Don't be absurd. Not everything we use explodes," Mr. Murphy said.

I guess I had no reason not to trust him. And it wasn't like my situation could get any worse. Even so, I hesitated.

The woman smiled at me. "Relax, hon. It won't hurt." She was pretty, with short dark hair and brown eyes. "We're just going to use a light test dosage. It will strengthen your fingers, but only for a little while. I can't do your whole body until I finish upgrading the power supply."

I put my hand in the container.

"Go ahead, Dr. Cushing," Mr. Murphy said.

Dr. Cushing went to a small refrigerator in one corner and took out a carton of milk. She filled the container, covering my hand. Then she pushed some buttons and turned a large black dial. I heard a deep hum. The sound rose to a whine. My hand started to tingle. My fingers felt warm, and then hot—but not so hot that they hurt. It was actually sort of nice. Tiny bubbles rose from the milk. The feeling, and the hum, lasted for a minute or two. Then they both faded. It was weird having any sort of pleasant feeling.

Dr. Cushing pointed to the sink. "You can take your hand out now."

I pulled my hand from the milk and washed it off.

"Check out your fingers," Mr. Murphy said.

I grabbed my right little finger and bent it a little. It didn't snap off. I bent it harder. It was as strong as it used to be.

"This is great," I said. That was the worst part of my zombie condition. Things broke too easily. I tried not to think about it too much. Now, it looked like there was hope. "You can do this to my whole body?"

Mr. Murphy nodded. "Absolutely. As soon as you agree to work for us and let us run some tests."

"So, if I don't work for you, you won't help me?" I asked.

He shrugged. "Sorry. That's how it is. We might strive for the good of the free world, but we aren't a charity."

I actually kind of liked the idea of being a spy. Though I definitely didn't want to smuggle documents inside my body. And I still thought superheroes were a lot cooler. "If I agree to work for you, what happens next?"

"First, we need to run some tests. We want to find out about your abilities. You must already know some of them, but there might be much more to discover. What do you say? Are you the newest member of BUM? Imagine how exciting it will be. I'll even let you play with the squirrels."

As much as I wanted them to strengthen my bones, I didn't want to give him an answer before I talked with Mookie and Abigail.

I looked at the machine that had zapped my hand, and tried to memorize as much of a description as I could. It was made up of four different parts. There was some stuff written on the side of the parts. Abigail might know what it all meant. If BUM could strengthen my bones, maybe someone else could, too.

"Can I have some time to think about it?" I asked.

"Certainly," he said. "But don't take too long. If you're already breaking fingers, your arms and legs aren't too far behind."

"We'll need time to set up the tests, anyhow," Dr. Cushing said.

"Monday?" Mr. Murphy asked her.

She nodded.

"Come here after school," Mr. Murphy said. "Unless you decide you're better off without our help." He made a choking sound. It took me a moment to realize he was holding back a laugh.

"What's so funny?" I asked.

"I had an impulse to say something else, but I realized it was totally tasteless."

"Don't let that stop you," I said. "I like tasteless stuff as much as you like exploding squirrels."

"Well, all right. If you turn us down and your leg breaks off, don't come crawling back to me."

He chuckled. Dr. Cushing shook her head and sighed.

"Not bad," I said. Despite his weirdness, I thought I might actually be able to get along with him.

He walked me back to the elevator. I sat and had another rocket ride, returning to the lobby at the Museum of Tile and Grout.

"What happened," Mookie asked when I met back up with him and Abigail at the Gas 'n' Snack.

I told them everything. After I described the machine to Abigail, I asked her, "Do you have any idea what it is?"

"I think so. It sounds like a modified neutron beam." She paused, then smacked her forehead and said, "Of course! Why didn't I think of that? They're running it through a splitter, and then setting one half out of phase. The dissonance forces the cells to absorb calcium. You get it?"

"Not at all."

"That's okay. At least we know the technology exists to strengthen your bones."

"Is there a machine like it anywhere else?" I asked. I figured if things didn't work out with BUM, maybe I could go somewhere else to strengthen my bones. I kind of liked the idea of being a spy, but I didn't like feeling that I had no choice.

"Not anywhere around here," Abigail said. "They might have something like it at Fermi Lab, or CERN."

"Now you're just making up names to impress us," Mookie said.

Abigail ignored him.

"Could you build one?" I asked.

"Sure," Abigail said. "If I had ten or fifteen thousand dollars for the parts.

"Whoa," Mookie said. "That's a whole lot of money."

"It's a lot of parts," Abigail said.

"I guess I just have to agree to work for them," I said. "That should be okay."

"You don't even know what they want you to do," Abigail said.

"I'll find out soon enough." I flexed my strengthened fingers, then gave Mookie a hard poke. It would be great if all my bones were this strong again.

12

▼

Winging It

Mookie showed up at my door at noon on Saturday. "Your problems are solved," he said. "You can start saving up for your own bone machine. You're going to make a ton of money today. Abigail isn't the only one with great ideas."

"What are you talking about?"

He held up a folded newspaper and pointed to an ad. "There's a hot-wing-eating contest this afternoon at the new supermarket. You can win it easy."

"But I don't eat."

"You don't *need* to eat. But you *can* eat. And you won't get sick or anything. You'll be able to stuff your gut a lot better than anyone else. How cool is that?"

"I'm too skinny," I said.

"Are you kidding? Have you seen those champion hot dog eaters? They make you look like a blob. They're totally thin."

"I don't know." I thought about the last time I'd forced food out of my stomach. It hadn't been fun.

"I've got two words for you," Mookie said.

"What?"

"Five hundred dollars."

"That's three words."

"No, it isn't," Mookie said. "The dollars part isn't a word. It's that ess thing with the lines through the middle." He stuck out two fingers and drew lines in the air.

"It's a word if you say it."

"It's also first prize."

"We need at least ten thousand dollars for the parts to make one of those machines," I said.

"So after we win this, we'll only need like . . ." He counted on his fingers for a moment or two, then shrugged and said, "Five hundred dollars less."

"It just doesn't sound like a good idea."

"Come on. It will be awesome. You're a winner, Nate. Haven't you noticed? You're winning everything these days."

I figured there wouldn't be any real harm in eating some hot wings. And he was right. Five hundred dollars was a lot of money. "Okay. I'll do it."

"Great. This is just the start, you know. I'll bet there are all sorts of ways a zombie can make money."

"I'm not a zombie."

"Hey, that reminds me of a joke. What's a zombie's favorite weather forecast?"

"I don't know."

"Cloudy with a chance of brain."

"That's not funny."

"Yes, it is. Hey—brain showers! That's totally hilarious." To prove he was right, he started laughing.

Mookie was still laughing when we reached Van Houghton Street, where the new SortaFresh Discount Supermarket had opened last week. There were a couple tables set up in a corner of the parking lot with folding chairs behind them, and more folding chairs lined up in front of them for spectators.

A short line of people were there already, waiting to sign up for the contest. Short—but very wide. Most of them had huge stomachs. I felt like a toothpick wandering among beach balls. When I reached the table, the guy in charge stared at me for a minute. "You know this line is for the hot-wing eating contest?"

"I know."

The guy shrugged and pushed the clipboard toward me. I wrote down my name, address, and age, then took a seat and waited for the contest to start. It looked like there were about twenty people, including one guy who must have weighed close to four hundred pounds.

The judges placed a plate of wings in front of each of us, along with a big glass of water.

Mookie took a seat in the front row. "Don't drink

anything. That will just take up room. Concentrate on the chicken."

"Good idea." When they rang the starting bell, I grabbed a wing, bit off the meat from one side, and swallowed it without chewing. I figured that would save time. I glanced at the guy next to me. He was already on his second wing—which wasn't surprising, since he was grabbing them two at a time. I'd have to hurry to keep up.

It felt strange to eat—especially since my taste buds had been sort of numbed ever since I'd been splashed with Hurt-Be-Gone. But I got a bit of the flavor. Even if I hadn't been able to taste the wings at all, I could tell they were hot from the groans and screams that rose around me.

I tuned all of that out and concentrated on eating. Soon enough, my first plate was empty. By now, I was about even with the guy next to me. I guess he'd slowed down. They put another plate in front of me. I kept biting and swallowing. Out of the corner of my eye, I saw someone get up and stagger away from the table.

I realized I wasn't sweating, either. Hot sauce used to make me sweat.

By the third plate, the guy next to me was still going, but I could tell I was beating him. The big guy two seats away had a stack of empty plates. I kept at it until the bell rang again.

"Time!" someone shouted.

I dropped the half-eaten wing I was holding, wiped my hands on a paper towel, and slumped back in my seat.

As I did that, my pants popped open. The button shot off and smacked against the edge of the table. I stared down at my gut. It was bulging pretty badly. But that was okay. I'd force all that chicken out of my stomach soon enough.

The judges moved from person to person, weighing all the plates and writing stuff down on clipboards.

Mookie came up to me right after they left. "You were awesome."

"Thanks. Anyone else eat this much?"

"No way. Nobody came close." He pointed to the judges' table. "Hang on—I think they're going to announce the winner."

A guy wearing a SortaFresh apron picked up a microphone. "Okay, folks, the results are in. We have winners to announce."

He walked toward me. I could already feel the money in my hands. I wondered whether they'd give it to me in hundred-dollar bills.

"With a total of sixty-three wings, Nathan Abercrombie wins the youth division and a twenty-five-dollar SortaFresh gift certificate."

"What?" I shouted. *Youth division?*

He ignored me and walked over to the four hundred-pound guy. "And our adult division winner, with a total of fifty-seven wings, is Bubba 'Big Gut' Chompsketski. Let's have a hand for him."

People clapped. The manager handed Bubba a check. I jumped out of my seat. That is, I tried. The extra weight in my gut slowed me down and threw me off balance so my jump was more like a lurch and a stumble.

"That's not fair!" I shouted at the manager. "I beat him."

The manager shrugged and tapped some stuff written at the bottom of the entry form. "Rules are rules, kid. Come back when you're eighteen."

"Hey, look on the bright side," Mookie said. "At least you got twenty-five dollars."

"Yeah, in a stinking gift certificate. Come on—let's get this chicken out of me."

I took two steps, then clutched at my pants as they fell. Luckily, I caught them before they hit the ground. Unluckily, they'd dropped as far as my knees. I yanked them up, then handed Mookie the gift certificate. "Go see if they sell rope, or belts, or something."

"You bet." Mookie snatched the certificate from my hand and dashed into the store.

As I sat and waited, a shadow fell over me from the side. Something was blocking the sun.

"You did good, kid."

I looked up. "Thanks."

Bubba swatted me on the back with a meaty paw that was pretty heavily covered in hot sauce. "You could really make a name for yourself. It's not just wings. There's a whole lot of contests out there. Oysters, pies, pizza, deep-fried onions . . ." He let out a small burp, licked his lips, then said, "Well, I'll see you around."

It was at least fifteen more minutes before Mookie came back, carrying a bulging plastic bag.

"They have belts?" I asked.

"Nope. But they had pet stuff. I got you a leash." He pulled it out of the bag and handed it to me.

"Thanks." I threaded the leash through my belt loops, then tied it. "What's in there?"

"I got us a snack for later." Mookie opened the bag and showed me a bunch of chocolate bars, pretzels, and licorice whips.

"I'm not eating anything else," I said. "I don't eat food anymore. Remember."

"Oops. Sorry. I forgot. That's okay, I'll eat them for you. That's what friends are for."

"Speaking of eating—come on. Let's get this stuff out of me."

I took a step and watched to make sure my pants wouldn't fall. They stayed up, but they looked like they were ready to burst.

We walked over to the playground behind Borloff Lower Elementary School. The way my gut was pulling me, I felt I was going downhill the whole time. When we were halfway there, a bird swooped down toward me, aimed right at my head. *Oh no, not another BUM spy going out of control.*

"Duck!" I shouted.

Mookie and I ducked. Or at least, I ducked as much as I could with a gut full of wings. The bird shot past me and hit the trunk of a tree. As it dropped to the ground, I realized I hadn't heard a clang.

"I think it's real," I said. The bird shook its head like it was dazed, flapped its wings, and flew off, zigzagging through the air.

"Definitely weird," Mookie said.

"But definitely not a spy from BUM," I said.

When we got to the monkey bars, I climbed up a couple rungs, then hung down from my knees.

"Get it over with," I said.

Mookie leaned forward and pressed against my stomach. I opened my mouth wide so the food could shoot out more easily.

"Nothing's happening," Mookie said.

"Press harder"

"Urrrfff." Mookie leaned into me. I could tell he was using all his strength.

"I think it's stuck." He dropped his arms and staggered away from me.

"No. It can't be stuck." I imagined all that chicken jammed in my stomach. Sixty-three wings. "Try again."

It didn't work any better the second time.

"It's no use." Mookie's face was red, and sweat ran down his cheeks. He looked like he was the one full of hot wings. I guess he'd really given it a hard try.

"We'd better call Abigail," I said. "She'll know what to do."

13

▼

Gut Instincts

"This doesn't sound good," Abigail said. "Meet me at my place."

Abigail's place was the Comfy Craven Motor Lodge and Bait Shop, on Route 49 right outside of town. She and her mom were staying there while they waited to move into their new house.

Mookie and I cut through the field by the mall, which got us to a road that ran behind the motel. We walked around to the front, where a long row of doors stretched out from the office. Abigail was in number fifteen.

"This is so cool," Mookie said when Abigail answered our knock. "I love motels."

"Me, too. I feel like Eloise," Abigail said.

Mookie and I stared at each other. I didn't have a clue.

"Eloise is from a picture book," Abigail said. "She lives in the Plaza Hotel. That's not important right now. We need to deal with this."

She reached out and poked my stomach. "Ohmygosh. What did you eat?"

"Sixty-three chicken wings," I said.

"They're sort of jammed in there," Mookie said.

"Did you forget to chew?" Abigail asked.

"There wasn't really time," I told her. "I was afraid Bubba would beat me."

"Bubba?" Abigail asked.

"He lives in the Plaza Hotel," Mookie said.

Abigail ignored him. "We need to liquefy the food."

"How are we going to do that?" I asked.

"I know!" Mookie said. "My mom bought this thing from the TV shopping channel. It's like a blender on a stick. You put it in a pot of food and make soup. She makes all kinds of soup now. We had hot dog and relish soup last week. Anyhow, we could stick it down your throat."

"Right—and blend my guts into soup. No thank you." I hoped Abigail had a better idea.

She tugged at the ends of her hair and looked up toward the clouds. I waited. Finally, she said, "Normally, stomach acid does the trick. Along with saliva. I suspect you aren't producing any stomach acid."

"Can we get some?" Mookie asked.

"We could," Abigail said. "We could even make something like it in a chem lab. But that would be dangerous. A living stomach can protect itself against acid. Otherwise it would digest itself. But I don't think Nathan's stomach is producing any protection. The acid would eat right through it, and then through the rest of his body."

"That doesn't sound good." I pictured acid burning holes through my stomach and running down my legs. Even if I couldn't feel any pain, I definitely didn't want to give birth to a pile of chicken wings.

"You're right—it wouldn't be good at all," Abigail said. "But there are gentler ways to deal with proteins. We can use enzymes. Meat tenderizer would be a good start. And papaya extract."

Abigail ran inside, tore a piece of paper out of her notebook, and started writing. After a minute, she said, "Come on. We've got some shopping to do."

"I just went shopping," Mookie said. He held up the bag. "Have some chocolate."

Now Abigail heard him loud and clear. She reached into the bag and pulled out a bar.

"Brain food," she said.

"Brains—yum." Mookie shoved a chocolate bar toward my face. "Mmmmm. Zombie boy likes brains."

I pushed his hand away. "Knock it off."

"Okay, I'll eat your brains." Mookie chomped down on the bar. Then he started to laugh.

"Okay, what is it?" I asked.

"I got another one. How does a zombie measure stuff?"

"I don't know."

"With a twelve-inch drooler."

"That's not funny," I said.

"Yes, it is."

He laughed and ate all the way back to the market. I stayed behind him so I wouldn't get sprayed with chocolate goop.

After finding everything on her list, Abigail said, "Okay. We just have to mix it up and let you drink it. In a week or so, all the meat will be pretty much liquified. Then you can hang upside down and drain it right out of you."

"That would be perfect." I really didn't like lugging around all the extra weight. I was definitely off balance. I wasn't used to having a gut hanging down in front of me.

We went to my place, and Abigail mixed up the formula. After I drank it down, she had me drink a couple large glasses of water.

"The more liquid you can add to the mix, the better," she said. "Try to keep drinking a lot each day."

I patted my stomach. "I'll do whatever it takes to get rid of this." The water made me feel even heavier. But I didn't care, since I knew it would all be out of me soon enough.

"Just be careful," Abigail said. "The decomposition might produce a bit of methane. That's an explosive gas. Keep away from flames and sparks."

Mookie laughed and poked me in the gut. "Boom!"

over by the bleachers,
all run.

A loud buzz echoed
board timer reached zero
the weights, after every
out, but also run twenty
me. And Rodney was gla

I groaned, then let m
was tired. I put down the
first lap.

"No need, Abercrom
the distance. You earne
walked over to me, then

"Do you see? This is
member what this boy
year? He was a total mess
even run a lap without g
in shape. And do you kn

"I know!" Mookie
the air. Then his eyes
"No, I don't!" He shook
down.

Everyone else shook
clue.

"Because I drove h
thumped his chest. "Me
champion athlete. That
I can do that for all of yo

By then, it was time for class. We learned about Nathan Hale in social studies. He was hanged by the British during the Revolutionary War for being an American spy. I hoped this wasn't a pattern for Nathans.

"Good thing you don't need to breathe," Mookie whispered to me as Ms. Otranto finished the lesson.

In gym class, every pair of wrestlers except for Rodney and Omar had joined Ferdinand and me in pretending to wrestle. We did perfect takedowns, perfect escapes, and all sorts of other awesome moves. Kids flashed me grins or winks whenever Mr. Lomux wasn't watching.

"All right," he said halfway through class. "You're not looking bad. Let's toughen you kids up some more."

He had each of us grab a pair of dumbbells and hold our arms straight out to the side. Then he set the timer on the basketball scoreboard to fifteen minutes.

"Whoever drops his arms before time runs out gives me twenty laps," he said.

I heard grunts and groans around me. In a minute or two, there were kids running laps. I watched Mookie run. He flapped his arms and pretended he was a bird. Mr. Lomux yelled at him. Mookie didn't seem to care.

I had the feeling Mookie would be able to deal with being a zombie a lot better than I could. He seemed to be able to handle everything that happened in his life.

I realized the gym was a lot quieter than it had been. There weren't any footsteps. Nobody was running. I guess I'd gotten lost in thought. I looked around. Everyone was over by the bleachers, catching their breath. They'd all run.

A loud buzz echoed through the gym as the scoreboard timer reached zero. Oh, great. I was still holding the weights, after every other kid had not only dropped out, but also run twenty laps. Mr. Lomux was staring at me. And Rodney was glaring.

I groaned, then let my arms drop, trying to pretend I was tired. I put down the barbells, then started to run my first lap.

"No need, Abercrombie," Mr. Lomux said. "You went the distance. You earned the right to skip the laps." He walked over to me, then turned to the class.

"Do you see? This is what I can do for you. Do you remember what this boy was like at the beginning of the year? He was a total mess. He was a weakling. He couldn't even run a lap without gasping. But look at him now. He's in shape. And do you know why?"

"I know!" Mookie shouted, thrusting his hand in the air. Then his eyes got wide and his face got pale. "No, I don't!" He shook his head and yanked his hand down.

Everyone else shook their heads. They didn't have a clue.

"Because I drove him hard," Mr. Lomux said. He thumped his chest. "Me. I turned a pathetic loser into a champion athlete. That's what they pay me to do. And I can do that for all of you."

As we headed out of class, Ferdinand said, "Wow—I never realized Mr. Lomux was such a good teacher."

In language arts, Ms. Otranto said, "This morning, in social studies, we learned about Nathan Hale. I want you to think about what he did. Then I want you to make some notes for an essay. The topic will be, *What does it mean to make a sacrifice for someone else?*"

That was a topic I already knew something about. But my experience wasn't the sort I wanted to put down in writing. It was something I wanted to feel again. I ended up just using some of the examples from social studies, but my mind kept flashing pictures of me running through the night in my superhero costume.

In art class, things went well.

"Very nice, Nathan."

"Huh?" I glanced up. Mr. Dorian was standing right next to me, looking down at my drawing.

"You have a good, steady line going there," he said. "Not everybody can control the pencil that perfectly."

"Uh, thanks." I looked at my drawing. Then I looked next to me, at Caleb's drawing, and understood what Mr. Dorian meant. Caleb's lines were sort of shaky. I checked out the rest of the drawings at our table. Denali's was pretty good, but the other three were even worse than Caleb's.

It was easy enough to understand what was happening.

This was one of the reasons I was so good at video games now. My hand didn't shake. It moved when I wanted it to move. It stayed still when I wanted it to stay still. I didn't shake, tremble, quiver, or twitch.

I didn't even shake when I headed off to BUM for my tests.

Top Secret

I'm glad you decided to join us, Nathan," Mr. Murphy said after I stepped out of the elevator. He put his arm on my shoulder.

"I still don't know what you want me to do," I said.

He led me to the TV room. "I think this will answer some of your questions."

A video started playing. "Welcome to BUM," a man in a gray suit said. He was standing in front of a building that looked like a castle.

"As a new recruit, you are one of a rare few who are lucky enough to have special abilities. We'll be making good use of those skills." The camera pulled back to show an eagle gliding across a clear blue sky above the castle.

"BUM has a crucial mission. We protect people who can't protect themselves. We make the world safe for freedom. We fight for things worth fighting for. We take things that are wrong and make them right."

He talked for another fifteen minutes. Maybe I just didn't know how to listen, but it really seemed like he didn't say anything.

When the film ended, Mr. Murphy turned off the TV. "Okay. I trust that answered many of your questions. Now, let me hand you off to Dr. Cushing so she can start the tests."

He led me back to her room. "Relax," she said. "None of this will be scary." She had me sit in a chair and then took my temperature, using one of those thermometers you stick in your ear.

"Hmmmm," she said. "Two degrees Celsius above ambient room temperature. Interesting. There must be a slight amount of metabolic activity."

I had the feeling Abigail would like her. I pointed to the bone machine. "How long until it's ready to do my whole body?"

"It should be all set by Friday," she said. "I'm just waiting for a couple parts I need to strengthen the beam."

"That will be great."

She took a needle from a drawer. "This will only hurt a bit."

"Actually, it won't hurt at all," I said.

She held up a hand to stop me. "Don't tell me anything about your abilities yet. I need to make sure these first tests are unbiased. If I know what you can do, it might influence my observations. Tomorrow, after I've had a chance to analyze my results, I want you to come back and tell me all about yourself."

She got a sample of my blood. That wasn't easy, since my heart doesn't beat. My blood just kind of stays in my veins. But she managed to get a little bit, which she said was all she needed. Even though it didn't hurt, I still looked away when she stuck me with the needle.

Then she brushed a liquid on my arm. "Allergen," she explained before I could ask, "I want to see if your body reacts to irritation."

Then you should bring Mookie here.

A phone on the wall rang. She picked it up, listened, then said. "Sure. I'll get you the sample." Then she turned to me. "Sorry, I have to run something down the hall. I'll be right back."

As I was waiting, a man walked past, pushing a hand cart piled with boxes. They looked familiar. I got out of my chair and peeked out of the room. The man went all the way down to the end of the corridor, and then through a door. A moment later, he came back out with the empty cart.

"What was that?" I asked when he walked past me.

"Surplus," he said.

Dr. Cushing came back before I could ask anything else.

"Let's check that arm," she said.

I sat back down. She looked at my arm with a huge

magnifying glass, then scraped a small skin sample and put it in a glass tube. "No apparent reaction," she said, typing some notes on a laptop computer.

After that, she tested my hearing. "More acute than normal," she said. "As I expected."

"Huh?"

"You have extra-sensitive hearing. Most people don't notice the noise, but blood is flowing through their heads. That masks some sounds. But your blood doesn't flow, so you hear better."

"That's sort of cool." I added super hearing to my list of powers. Maybe that would allow me to find people who were screaming for help.

She ran a series of other tests, then said, "That's plenty for one session. I'll see you tomorrow."

I got up and headed for the elevator. I noticed that she didn't offer to walk me there. I guess they trusted me.

On the way around the corner to meet up with Abigail and Mookie, I saw two more birds flying like they were out of control. One hit a house. The other tried to land on a phone line and missed it completely. It was definitely strange, but I had more important things on my mind.

"Remember that chemistry set your mom gave you?" I asked when I got there.

"My mom's given me thirteen chemistry sets," Abigail said. "Fourteen, if you count the one where all the bottles were empty. She scavenges things. But she's been really good since we moved to the motel."

"This was right after we took that hike in the woods," I said. I remembered the whole thing pretty well. It happened while Abigail was trying to make the cure for me. "Little Genius?"

"Oh, that one. Yeah. Little Genius Chemistry Set. I got rid of it right away. It was completely dangerous. It had radium in it and mercury."

"Yeah—you'd told us it was dangerous. Here's the problem—I think I saw a stack of them at BUM. They put them in some kind of storeroom."

"That doesn't make any sense," Abigail said. "What else was in the room?"

"I don't know," I said. "I didn't have a chance to look inside."

"This isn't good," Abigail said. "We need to find out what they've got in there. That could help us figure out what BUM is really doing. It's time to spy on the spies."

That night, I spent some time drawing. It was nice, but I didn't think it was the hobby I was looking for.

The next morning, as I pushed around my cereal, I heard my stomach growl.

"You're getting quite an appetite," Mom said.

"It's a big one," I said. I hoped all that chicken would hurry up and become mushy enough so I could get it out of my stomach. I looked silly with my pants pushed down below my gut. But at least my shirt sort of hid things a little.

All day Tuesday, the only thing I could think about was that I'd be going back to BUM and that, according to Abigail, I needed to do some spying of my own.

When I got there, Dr. Cushing was all set for my second session. This time, she had me tell her everything that had changed since I'd become a zombie. I showed her that I didn't need to breathe.

"Very useful," she said. "Between that and the minimal body temperature, there are so many potential ways we could use you."

"Thanks. I guess."

She put her hand on my shoulder. "It's good to make use of your skills. I know you didn't ask for this to happen. But you'll be helping a lot of people. It's okay to feel proud about that."

A couple minutes later, she got another phone call. As soon as she left, I slipped down the hall to the room at the end of the corridor.

It was a storage room. I saw a stack of the chemistry sets. They were definitely the same kind that Abigail had tossed. I went deeper and checked the shelves. There were some toys, games, and books. I recognized one of the books. I'd read it last year. It was about a kid who was always fooling around with batteries. I almost took apart an old car battery after that, but dad caught me and explained how there was acid and stuff inside.

I'd seen what I needed. I went back to the other room and waited for Dr. Cushing.

"That's all," she said as she finished up her tests. "We're done."

"Great." I hurried out and met back up with my friends.

"There's a lot of dangerous stuff in the storeroom," I told Abigail. "Why would they have it?"

She started to look up, but she didn't even get halfway there before her eyes grew wide and her mouth dropped open. "Ohmygosh!"

"What?"

"I don't think they're just looking for kids who've messed up," she said. "I think they're helping kids mess up."

"I mess up enough without help," Mookie said.

"Nobody would do something that awful," I said.

"Yes, they would," Abigail said. "History is full of stuff like that."

"They want to help people," I said. "I watched this whole movie about it. BUM isn't evil. They're good. They're going to help me. They know lots of stuff about the corpse flower."

"Oh-double-gosh!" Abigail said. Her eyes got wider.

"What?" I asked.

"The corpse flower isn't allowed into the country," she said. "So how did Uncle Zardo get it? Something rotten is going on here."

"And here," Mookie said, pointing to my stomach.

"Can we get in touch with him?" I asked Abigail. "I'm sure we'll find out BUM had nothing to do with it."

"He's still on Bezimo Island, but he's got an Internet phone."

"So does my dad," I said.

"Great," Abigail said. "We can call Uncle Zardo from your house."

We went to my place and got on the computer. Abigail made the call to her uncle.

"Hello, Twinkle," he said.

Mookie snickered. She kicked him in the shin. Then she said, "Uncle Zardo, you used the wrong ingredient in the formula. Instead of the corpus flower, you used the corpse flower. Because of that, the Hurt-Be-Gone turned my friend into a zombie."

"Oh, dear. That's unfortunate. How's he doing?"

"Better than you might expect for a dead kid," Abigail said. "But we have a question. We were wondering how you got the corpse flower. It's not legal to import it."

"I know. I tried to get it and I failed. And then a package arrived at the lab."

"Who brought the package?" I asked.

"Strange man," Uncle Zardo said. "He had a funny accent. And peculiar ears."

"Mr. Murphy," I whispered as Abigail said good-bye to her uncle and hung up.

Abigail and I looked at each other. "It's not my imagination," she said. "They made it happen."

"That's awful," Mookie said.

I felt like I'd been stabbed in the back. "No way I'm

doing anything for them. Forget BUM. They can find another zombie to be their spy."

"No, Nathan," Abigail said. "You have to let them give you the treatment. You need to get your bones strengthened. You can quit after that. And we can expose them to the world. You'll be a real hero for doing that. Think of all the kids you'll save."

She was right. I needed the treatment. And BUM needed to be exposed. After I got my bones taken care of, I could tell the world what BUM was doing. That would shut them down forever.

15
▼

Would You Like flies with That?

How long do you think we're going to be wrestling?" Adam asked as we walked toward gym class on Wednesday.

"Forever, I hope," Ferdinand said. "It's the first thing we've ever done in gym where I didn't get hurt."

"Good stuff never lasts," Mookie said. "We'll probably have to do something stupid next, like square dancing with the girls."

"I'd rather rip my arms off," Adam said.

Mookie and I looked at each other, but neither of us said anything.

When we got to the gym, Mr. Lomux said, "I have great news for all of you. Since this class has done such an amazing job wrestling, I've arranged an exhibition at the high school. It took a lot of work, but I didn't mind. You'll be wrestling right after the varsity match on Saturday night. And that's just the beginning."

"Cool," Adam said. "They've got an awesome gym."

"Ravens rule!" Rodney shouted.

"This sounds dangerous," Ferdinand said.

Mookie sighed. "There goes the weekend."

"I've invited the whole school board to come," Mr. Lomux said. "I want them to see the amazing progress you've made, thanks to my training methods. I'm expecting great things from some of you."

He pointed right at me. "When they see the way I've whipped you kids into shape, I'll be able to ask them for anything I want. We'll have the most awesome gym class in the state. I'll turn all of you into champion athletes. We won't stop at wrestling. We'll do this for every sport."

When the full meaning of that sank in, it seemed to kill some of the excitement in the bleachers. As much as I figured most of my classmates would enjoy wrestling in front of a crowd, the rest of it sounded like it was going to be a major pain.

I forgot all about that at lunch, when the swarm of flies invaded. At first, I just heard screams. Then a couple kids at another table jumped up and started swatting at the air.

Flies—it looked like hundreds of them—swarmed into the cafeteria. They flew toward our table. I was about to start swatting when a bunch of them landed in front of me. I stared at the table. The flies had formed a word.

NATHAN!

They flew off the table, then flew back.

URGENT!

I looked out the window. There was a familiar figure across the street. Mr. Murphy, dressed like a mailman, was holding some sort of small box.

By then, the flies had formed a different message:

435 CALAGARY ST.

And finally:

AS SOON AS YOU CAN.

The flies rose from the table and flew out of the cafeteria. They buzzed down the hall and turned toward the front door. A couple of them hit the wall, making tiny explosions like baby firecrackers.

I looked around. Nobody else had noticed the message, except Abigail.

"I guess I'd better go," I said.

She nodded. "Yeah, you'd better. But please be careful."

Right after school, I headed for Calagary Street and looked for number 435. As I was checking the street numbers, I saw a cat climbing a tree. Halfway up, it slipped and fell. It reminded me of the bird from the other day. It got up, then licked itself a couple times and acted like it had meant to fall. I watched it until I was sure it was all right, then headed down the block.

The door to the building was open. There was thick dust on the floor, and one set of footprints. Not a whole lot of light came through the dirty windows. Mr. Murphy was standing inside. Stacks of wooden crates filled a lot of the floor.

"Ever heard of e-mail?" I asked. "Or the telephone?"

He shrugged. "You have to admit, the flies were sort of impressive."

He had a point. "Why are we meeting here?"

"We live in dangerous times. I fear that BUM has been infiltrated by our enemies," he said. "I don't want them to know about you. You could very well be the greatest agent we've ever recruited."

Greatest agent? That was cool. But I was more interested in the other part. "What enemies?"

"There are various organizations that want to destroy our free society. They may already be aware of your existence. We could all be in danger. Let's sit. We need to go over everything you've noticed in the past week."

I followed him to a bench that was against one wall, and resisted the urge to ask him whether he was the one who was destroying things. Just as we were about to sit, I heard a scraping sound from the other side of a wall of crates.

"Stay here!" Mr. Murphy pushed me down and darted around the crates.

"Murphy!" someone shouted. "You're finished."

I heard a grunt, and a thud. There was a louder thump, and the wall of crates rocked like someone had slammed into it.

I got to my feet. There were more bangs and grunts, then a much louder crash. A couple crates toppled and fell on the other side.

I ran around. Mr. Murphy was on the ground. His legs were pinned under a crate. There was another guy sprawled out facedown. Between them, I saw a shiny box that was half shattered. A window in the wall was open. I guess the guy had come in that way.

I ran toward Mr. Murphy. He held up a hand. "Nathan, stop! That's a bomb."

I looked at the thing on the floor. It had colored wires in it, running to some sort of timer on one side. The number on the display was 00:47. A couple red sticks were taped to the other side.

"It's going to explode in less than a minute." He gasped and pressed one hand against his side. "Get out while you can."

"What about you?" I wasn't going to leave him. I glanced at the other guy. He wasn't moving.

"There's no time."

I reached toward the crate. "Maybe I can lift it off."

"Too heavy," he said. "Just go!"

"Can't I turn off the bomb?"

He shook his head. "One slip, and we'd both go up."

"I don't slip," I said. I knelt next to him. "What do I have to do?"

"Are you sure you want to try this?" he asked.

"Dead sure."

He pointed to a yellow wire. "You have to pull it from its clip and then guide it all the way out of the case. But you can't make the slightest mistake. If the bare end touches any of the metal parts, it's all over. As soon as it's out, you can yank the red wire. That will stop the timer."

I put my hand on the yellow wire. The case was split. I could see inside. The bare tip of the yellow wire was less than an eighth of an inch from the side. The display read 00:28.

I pinched the wire between my thumb and first finger, moving as gently as if I were picking up a butterfly.

"Steady, lad," Mr. Murphy said.

I started to inch the wire free.

The timer kept counting down. I could barely see light between the end of the wire and the side of the container.

I had it halfway out. I had no idea what would happen to me if I was blown to bits. And I really didn't want to find out.

The other guy groaned and raised his head. I couldn't believe my hand hadn't jerked. But I was rock solid. The guy started to crawl toward me.

I moved the wire as quickly as I could. The guy was just a foot away. The timer read 00:07.

I got the yellow wire out. Then I yanked the red one. The timer died at 00:02.

The guy got to his feet. He walked toward me and held his hand out.

Mr. Murphy reached out and took his hand. The guy pulled him to his feet. The crate rolled off him like it was made of balsa wood.

"Well done, Nathan," Mr. Murphy said.

The bad guy tucked in his shirt and ran a hand through his hair. "You free for lunch tomorrow, Peter?" he asked Mr. Murphy.

"Absolutely, Ralph," Mr. Murphy said. "Pasta Grossa at noon?"

"See you then." He walked off.

I grabbed Mr. Murphy's arm. "What was that all about?"

"A test," he said. "We had to make sure you wouldn't panic in the field."

"A test? Are you crazy?" I kicked the crate. It splintered like zombie fingers.

He shrugged. "Be happy. You passed. You have what it takes. And, I must say, I was quite pleased with my performance, too. It's not easy pretending to be hurt. Did you like the way I gasped? Was it convincing?"

"Don't ever do that to me again," I said.

"I won't."

"Promise."

He smiled. "You have my word."

All the way home, I bounced between being angry at him for tricking me, and proud of myself for being so calm.

"Dead calm," I whispered.

That made me smile.

I told Mookie and Abigail about the test the next morning.

"Cool," Mookie said. "Why can't we have tests like that in school? I'd definitely do better at math if there were more bombs."

"I'd imagine Nathan didn't think it was cool when it was happening," Abigail told him.

"I really didn't have time to think at all," I said.

"This is just more proof that you definitely can't trust them," Abigail said. "If they can do this sort of thing, they can do anything."

"At least Mr. Murphy promised there'd only be one test," I said. "So I guess I won't see him again until Friday."

I was wrong.

16

They're All Bats

That night, as I was getting ready for bed, something slammed into my window. I spun around and saw a bat pressed against the glass. It stayed there for a moment, then fluttered away.

There was a smudge on the window. It started to glow. I got closer, and saw writing: CHECK YOUR E-MAIL. As I stared at the words, they faded.

A second bat slammed into the window. It left a message, too: NOW!

I went downstairs. My parents were still awake. "Okay if I check something on the computer real quickly?"

"Is it for school?" Mom asked.

"It's for a test," I said. That was probably true.

"Go ahead."

I logged on and checked my e-mail. There was a message from Mr. Murphy:

Nathan,
I'm using e-mail, just as you requested. Though you must admit, the bats are impressive. Please meet me on the corner as soon as you can. This is not a test.

That was the whole message. I figured he just said this wasn't a test to trick me into taking another test. But I also wanted to get my bones strengthened. I guess there was also a part of me that wanted to show him I could handle whatever he threw at me. Right after my folks went to sleep, I slipped out my bedroom window and climbed onto the garage roof. From there, I was able to lower myself to the ground.

I saw a black car by the curb around the corner. As I reached it, the passenger window rolled down. From the driver's side, Mr. Murphy said, "Get in."

"What's this about?"

"A sudden opportunity."

I got in. "Are you sure this isn't another test?"

He stared at me and slowly shook his head. "This is the real thing. We just received information about a major threat to a large part of the population in this region of New Jersey."

We headed out of town, followed the highway for several miles, then turned onto a narrow road that ran through the woods. After a couple miles of twisty turns, Mr. Murphy switched off his headlights. The road ahead vanished in the darkness. He turned the steering wheel to the right.

I braced myself for a collision with a tree. But he rolled to a stop without hitting anything. Then he shut the engine and handed me a portable video player. "I have something to show you."

"Can't you just tell me my instructions?" I asked. "Do you have to do everything with gadgets?"

There was a long pause before he answered me. "These aren't instructions. This is evidence. It appears you've done a bit of snooping in our hallways."

As I opened my mouth to deny it, Mr. Murphy reached over and hit PLAY. The video showed me sneaking down the hallway to the storage room.

"Spying is admirable," he said. "This proves you have the sort of talent and attitude we need. You're sly, cunning, and deceptive." He smiled at me.

"Thanks." I figured there was more coming.

"But spying on us is definitely not admirable. We need to be able to trust you."

"You can trust me."

I wondered whether he'd brought me here to get rid of me. But all he said was, "I'll find out in a minute."

He didn't know I'd discovered BUM's secret. He had no idea that, thanks to Abigail, I knew how dangerous those chemistry sets were. I was safe for now—as long as

I did what he asked. He got out and pulled a large bag from the trunk.

I joined him.

"Do you see that building?" He pointed to our left.

We were right next to a fence. It was hard to tell in the dark, but the fence must have been twenty or thirty feet high. In the darkness of the woods, I could make out a large building on the other side. It didn't seem to have any windows. I started to lean against the fence.

"Whoa there, cowboy." Mr. Murphy grabbed my wrist. "It's electrified. That's why I brought you. We need to get someone over to the other side."

"Can't you send one of your robots?"

He shook his head. "The electric field disrupts their control systems. This is a job for a person. But the electricity can stop a living person's heart. So we need a person without a heartbeat. Does that sound like anyone we know?"

I tried to remember everything I'd learned about electricity in science class. "Won't I get burned?"

"Probably not."

"Probably?" I'd been hoping for *definitely* or *absolutely*.

"High voltage causes burns. This fence has low voltage but high amperage. It's specifically designed to keep people from climbing it. Trust me, Nathan—you're the only one who can do this. And it has to be done tonight. Every second could make a difference."

"So, what am I doing?"

He handed me a small backpack. "There's a package in here. Once you clear the fence, go around to the back of the building. You'll see three exhaust vents. Slip the package through the opening in the center vent, and your mission is done. Come back, and I'll take you home."

"What if I don't want to do this?"

"It's a long walk."

"You wouldn't leave me here, would you?" I waited for an answer. The silence told me all I needed to know.

Mr. Murphy dropped a rubber doormat by the fence. "Stand on this. It will insulate you from the ground so you can get started. Do your shoes have rubber soles?"

"Yup." I wasn't sure why I needed to be insulated if the electricity couldn't hurt me. But I figured he wasn't going to answer any more questions. I slipped my arms through the straps and put on the backpack. Then I reached up with my right hand and grabbed the fence. I expected to feel some sort of jolt.

Nothing happened. I put my left foot on the fence and stepped up.

Nothing happened. I grabbed the fence with my other hand.

Something happened.

I guess I completed the circuit. As electricity ran through my arms, my fingers clamped down, making tight fists. My whole body twitched. I tried to say something, but my head was jerking around like a bobble-head doll in an earthquake.

Even my throat and lungs went out of control. Weird

screams shot out of me. "Wuuhwaahhhbwugaaaurrggga-zoo!!!!" I sounded like the world's worst screaming rock singer. Or maybe the best.

I remembered the frog in science class, twitching whenever it got jolted with electricity.

"Hang on," Mr, Murphy said. Then he giggled and added, "I guess there's no need to tell you that since you have to hang on. But, anyhow, be patient. The current will stop in a moment. It has to recharge."

Sure enough, after I'd done a bit more of my twitchy dance-and-scream song, my body suddenly went slack. I almost fell before I remembered to grab on. I looked back to tell Mr. Murphy how much I hated him, but he shouted, "Hurry! It recharges pretty quickly."

I scrambled higher. I was halfway up the fence when the second jolt hit me. Once again, I looked like a last-place contestant in a dance competition.

I got jolted two more times before I made it to the ground on the other side.

"Well done," Mr. Murphy said.

I glared at him. Then I headed for the building and went around back. Just like he said, there were three vents in the wall. I slipped off the backpack and took out the package. It was about the size and weight of a brick, but wrapped in plastic.

"Probably a brick," I muttered.

I pushed it through the center opening, then went back to the fence. I scrambled my way over, getting zapped several more times. Mr. Murphy was still there.

"Thanks for waiting," I said.

"You're valuable. Let's go."

We got in the car. He started the engine and switched on the headlights. When the light hit the fence, I saw a sign with a flag on it. An American flag.

GOVERNMENT PROPERTY
KEEP OUT

"What is this place? What was that all about?"

Mr. Murphy didn't answer me. Instead, he turned the car around and headed back the way we'd come. A moment later, I heard a huge boom. The sky behind us lit up and flames shot in the air.

I had a sudden suspicion I knew what was in that package.

"What did I just do?" I asked.

"You did what you were told."

"You made me blow up a building," I said. I could hear sirens now. *What did I do?*

"Nonsense. You didn't blow up the whole building. It was a very small explosion. You merely killed the power to the fence and sent a small signal."

"But . . ."

"No more questions. You need to decide whether you can trust me. And I need to know I can trust you. Think about what you've seen and done. Think carefully. Because once you join, we expect absolute loyalty. Forever."

We drove the rest of the way in silence. By the time I

got back to my room, I'd come up with dozens of crazy ideas to explain what I'd just done. But, whatever I'd blown up, I didn't like the idea that Mr. Murphy wouldn't tell me anything. And I really didn't like the idea that it was a government building.

Even though it was late, I called Abigail. I had to tell someone what had happened.

"Do you have any idea where you were?" she asked.

"No. We didn't cross the river, so I guess we were still in Jersey. We headed south on the highway for a couple miles, then took a twisty road. That's all I know. But I blew something up. What if I get sent to prison for life? I'll be there forever!"

"Calm down," Abigail said. "Take a deep breath."

"What good will that do?" I asked.

"Okay, good point. Forget the breath. But don't get all worried. I'll see if I can find out anything," she said. "There can't be that many government buildings that close to here. Either way, after tomorrow, you're done with BUM."

"I hope so."

17

▼

Large Scale Problems

When I got to school Friday morning, I saw Mookie and Adam over by the parking lot with Denali. She looked like she'd been crying.

"The shop?" I asked Mookie.

He nodded. "Her folks are about to give up."

"It's just too hard for them," Denali said between sniffles. "They're trying to open up at night, but business is so slow that they can't afford to hire any help. They have to do everything by themselves. So they're both exhausted all the time."

"That's rough." I thought about my dad, and how tired he seemed after a long day of work.

"They're ready to quit," she said. "They're running a

124

big ad in the paper today to try to get more business. If that doesn't work, it's over. We'll have to go live with my grandma and grampa. I don't want to move."

She started crying again. By then, Abigail had showed up.

"Find out anything?" I asked her.

"Not yet. I checked the whole area where you might have been, and compared it to a list of government properties. There are no active military bases or federal buildings around there like the one you described."

Abigail and Snail Girl went over and hugged Denali. I backed away with the rest of the guys. We could handle blood and vomit, but tears made us nervous.

I found something else to be nervous about after lunch. At the end of gym class, Mr. Lomux walked over to his office and dragged out the scale.

"All right," he bellowed. "Let's see who you're going to be grappling with. We want to make sure nobody is wrestling out of his weight class."

"Bring 'em on." Rodney rushed to be first. I was surprised that Omar rushed up, too. After Rodney was weighed, he stayed near the scale.

When Omar stepped on the scale, it turned out he'd lost nine pounds.

"Yes!" he said, pumping his fist in the air.

"Guess he won't be wrestling Rodney," Adam said.

"I hate this," Mookie said as he slipped in behind me. "I always think they're going to stop sliding that stupid little weight, but it keeps going."

I knew what Mookie meant. The little weight always moved too far along the crossbar for him. It never moved far enough for me.

Except this time.

When I stepped on the scale, the crossbar pasted itself against the top with a sharp clank.

"You've beefed up, Abercrombie," Mr. Lomux said. He slid the weight to the right, and kept sliding it. "I knew you'd put on some muscle if I trained you right."

The weight finally reached the balance point. Between the chicken wings and the water, I'd gained seventeen pounds. I looked down at my stomach. All that chicken and water were still in there.

Rodney made a snapping motion with his fists, like he was breaking a branch—or maybe a twig—in half. "He's mine."

"That's temporary weight." I pointed to my stomach. "It's mostly water. It will be gone before Saturday."

"Next!" Mr. Lomux shouted, ignoring me.

I stepped off the scale. Behind me, the crossbar slammed back down.

I waited for Mookie.

"I'm dead," I said when he joined me.

He nodded. "You're dead."

I imagined Rodney crushing me, or slamming me down so hard, all my bones broke.

Abigail was definitely right. I had to go to BUM to get my bones strengthened.

"Do you want us to come along?" she asked after school.

"I'll be fine," I said.

She nodded, but kept staring at me. "What's wrong?" I asked.

"I'm not sure. I have this nagging feeling there's something about the bone machine that I'm missing. I went over my calculations seven times. They seem fine. But my gut tells me I forgot to include an important factor. It's all kind of complicated. I'm pretty good with molecular biology, but particle physics isn't my strongest area. I wish you could wait a couple days before doing this."

I thought about Rodney and the way he'd smashed Omar to the mat. "I don't think that's a good idea."

"Yeah," Mookie said. "We don't want Nathan scattered across the gym like a ripped-open sack full of LEGOs."

Abigail nodded. "I understand. I'm sure it's nothing. I'll just go home and think about it a little more. Good luck."

"Thanks."

Luckily for me, Abigail was a quick thinker.

18

Porking Out

Last time I'm making this trip, I thought as I walked to the museum. I really wished BUM had turned out to be the good guys. I bet it would have been awesome going on spy missions.

On the way there, I saw a dog run into a fire hydrant. *Mookie's right*, I thought. *This town is definitely getting weirder.*

When I reached the front steps of the museum, I heard a scream.

"Wait! Nathan, wait!"

I spun around and saw Abigail racing down the street toward me on a bike. She hit the brakes, and went flying over the handlebars. Luckily, she landed on the grass.

"Are you okay?" I asked.

She nodded, gasping. I guess she was too out of breath to talk right away.

"Look, I need to get down to BUM."

She shook her head. "Dangerous."

I realized the best thing was for me to wait until she could talk. She sat up, took a couple deep breaths, then said, "I did more calculations. I think the bone machine is dangerous."

"So is wrestling Rodney," I said. "At least the bone machine won't rip off my head and shove it somewhere else."

"It could destroy you," she said.

I held up my hand and wiggled my fingers. "It worked fine the other day. I can tell it's wearing off, but my hand definitely got stronger for a while."

"That was a small dose. A lasting dose could do terrible things to your body."

"So you're telling me I shouldn't get my bones strengthened?" I didn't even want to think about that. Not after being so excited about the machine. "Are you absolutely positive about this?"

She started to nod. Then she frowned and said, "There's a small chance I'm wrong. You need to ask them to run a test first. That way, you'll know for sure."

She got up and brushed dirt off her knees.

"I didn't know you had a bike," I said.

"I borrowed it. I've never been on one before. The experience wasn't quite what I expected." She picked it up. "I think I'll walk it back."

"Thanks for coming."

"Sure. Good luck down there. I hope I'm wrong."

"I hope so, too."

"I called Mookie. We'll be waiting for you."

I watched her walk off, then went into the museum and took the elevator to BUM.

As Mr. Murphy walked with me to the lab, I tried to think of the best way to ask them to test the machine. Usually, adults don't like being told stuff by kids.

Dr. Cushing was eager to get started. "Ready for the treatment?" she asked me when I got to the lab.

"Almost." I noticed the table was gone and there was a big tub under the machine, filled with milk. "Are you sure it works?"

"Of course," Mr. Murphy said.

"Have you tested it?" I asked.

He turned and looked at Dr. Cushing. "Not really," she said.

"I think it would be a good idea to test it," I said.

"That's not necessary," Mr. Murphy said.

"It's good science," Dr. Cushing said. "Nathan is right. We shouldn't take chances. Give me a moment. I've got just what we need in the supply room."

She dashed out the door.

"A real spy would jump right in," Mr. Murphy said.

"Guess I'm not a real spy," I said.

"You are," he said. "You just need to start acting like one."

Dr. Cushing came back about five minutes later,

pushing a flat cart like the kind they have in the big hardware stores. There was a pig on it. A small dead pig.

"What's that?" I asked.

"Our test subject," she said. "It matches your weight pretty well."

"It's a pig," I said.

"Pigs are remarkably similar to humans in many ways," she said. "That why we always keep some on hand."

"It's dead," I said.

Dr. Cushing opened her mouth, then closed it.

"Right," I said. "So am I."

She turned to Mr. Murphy. "Help me put it in the vat."

They lifted the pig and put it in the milk. Then she turned a knob on the machine all the way to the right. "Here goes."

She pushed a button.

A hum came from the machine, starting low and then rising. The vat shook. The surface of the milk rippled. I saw a couple bubbles. Then I saw a lot of bubbles. The hum turned into a roar. The roar became a boom.

Everything exploded.

It was like someone had set off a stick of dynamite in the milk. It all blew up and shot out with a sound like a thousand pounds of cooked oatmeal getting dropped on the sidewalk from a mile in the air.

SPLAHBLAP!

Milk and pig pieces showered down on us. I was drenched with slop. I looked at my shirt. Slimy meat things were splattered all over it.

Dr. Cushing screamed.

I didn't blame her.

Mr. Murphy screamed, too.

"Thank you, Abigail," I whispered.

"I guess it's not quite ready," Dr. Cushing said.

"I guess I'll go home," I said. "Thanks for nothing."

"Nathan, wait," Dr. Cushing said. She put a hand on my shoulder. "I can get it to work. I know I can. Trust me."

"Trust you? No way! You can't help me. You can't fix anything. All BUM knows how to do is mess kids up. You're not making the world a better place. You're ruining it!" I spun away from her and headed into the hall.

She chased after me. "What are you talking about?"

"That!" I shouted, pointing toward the storage room. "All the stuff you make to mess kids up, like dangerous chemistry sets with radium." I barely managed to stop myself from screaming, *I'm telling!* I'd already revealed too much. I needed to get out of the building.

Past her, I saw Mr. Murphy slip his hand inside his jacket. I wondered how much damage a bullet would do to me. As I got ready to dive away, he pulled out a handkerchief and wiped his face. "Nathan, we didn't make those things. We collected them to get them away from young people like you."

"Then who made them?"

"I told you there are organizations that want to destroy our society."

"Yeah. And right after you told me that, a guy showed up with a fake bomb."

132

"The bomb was fake," Mr Murphy said. "Our enemies are real."

"I don't believe you," I said. "The person who gave Zardo Goldberg the corpse flower had a strange accent and peculiar ears."

"Well, there you go," Mr. Murphy said. "My ears are perfectly normal. And I don't have an accent."

"Yes, you do."

"I do not," he said. "You have a strange accent."

"What kind of accent was it?" Dr. Cushing asked me.

I opened my mouth to answer. Then I realized Abigail's uncle hadn't said what kind of accent. I'd just assumed it was Mr. Murphy who'd given him the corpse flower.

"It's a good idea to get all the facts before forming a conclusion," Dr. Cushing said.

I stared at her, halfway expecting her to morph into Abigail. I really liked Dr. Cushing, and I hated the fact that she was part of an organization that was hurting kids.

"I'm leaving." I walked down the hall, wondering whether anyone was going to stop me. That alone would be the proof I needed that BUM was evil and had things to hide.

"My ears are thoroughly average!" Mr. Murphy shouted.

But nobody chased after me.

19

The Parent Trap

I met up with my friends around the corner, by the Gas 'n' Snack convenience store. Abigail had bought a chocolate bar. Mookie, based on the evidence in the trash can next to him, was on his third pack of pretzel sticks.

He spat out a mouthful of half-chewed pretzels when he saw me. Then he pointed at my pig-splattered shirt and fell to the ground laughing.

"I take it the machine failed the test," Abigail said.

"Big time. If you hadn't warned me, Mr. Murphy and Dr. Cushing would be wearing pieces of me right now. I guess we're even. I saved you, and now you saved me. And I guess I'll never get my bones strengthened."

"We can worry about all that later," Abigail said. "Don't give up on the machine. But right now, we have something more important to deal with. We can't let you wrestle Rodney."

"No kidding," I said.

Mookie crawled back to his feet and held up a pretzel stick. "It wouldn't be pretty." He snapped the stick in half. "We'd need a lot of glue."

"Maybe the food is ready to come out," I said. Then I'd be back to my regular weight.

We went to the playground behind Borloff Elementary. A couple little kids stared at me when I hung down from the monkey bars. As soon as Mookie started pushing on my stomach, they giggled and raced over.

"Can we play?" they asked.

"Sure," Mookie said. "Push as hard as you can, but don't stand right under his face. He's going to spew big time."

They joined him, reaching toward me from the side and pressing their little hands against my big gut. It didn't do any good.

"It's not ready," Abigail said when I climbed back down.

"Is there any way to speed it up?" I asked.

"Heat, maybe. You should take a hot bath. And put a heating pad on your stomach when you go to bed. Just be careful. You don't want to build up too much pressure."

"At this point, I'll try anything."

I was dying to wash the pig bits off me, but I needed

to do something else first. I used the computer to call Abigail's uncle.

"The guy who brought you the corpse flower—what kind of accent did he have?"

"I couldn't place it," he said. "Maybe somewhere in Eastern Europe or the Mediterranean."

"Not British?" I asked. "Like on the vacuum cleaner infomercials?"

"Definitely not."

"Did he have red hair, big ears, and green eyes?" I asked.

"I believe he was bald with brown eyes," Abigail's uncle said. "I definitely remember his ears. They were tiny."

"Thanks." I hung up, then went to wash off my body and soak my bloated stomach in hot water. I wished I could soak my brain and wash away all the thoughts that kept drifting through it.

I spent so much time in the tub that night that Dad knocked on the door, asking if I was okay.

"I'm just relaxing," I said. "It's been a long week."

"I know it has, champ," Dad said. "Take your time."

Champ? He never called me that before. I wasn't going to try to guess what was going on. I had more important things to deal with. If I couldn't get rid of the food in my stomach, I needed to find a way out of the wrestling demonstration.

And I had to decide what to do about BUM. I still wasn't sure I trusted them. Just because Mr. Murphy hadn't given Abigail's uncle the corpse flower didn't mean someone else from BUM hadn't done it. They claimed they wanted to make the world a better place, but I hadn't seen a single thing that proved they did any good at all. And they'd tricked me into damaging a government building.

Before bedtime, I grabbed the heating pad from the closet. I stayed in bed and kept the pad on all night. I could hear all sorts of gurgling. I hoped it was working.

I got dressed as soon as it was light. I wanted to head over to the playground. I figured I could press on my stomach myself. Maybe the food was finally ready to come out.

Dad was in the kitchen with a cup of coffee. He had a bunch of papers spread out in front of him. I guess he'd gotten up early to do some work.

"Going out?" he asked.

"Yeah. I want to jog down to the playground," I said. That wasn't a lie. I liked jogging.

"Good for you. Have a nice run." He sounded a little sad.

"What's wrong?" I asked.

"I used to jog. There's nothing like a good run to clear your head. I haven't done that in ages."

"Want to come?" I figured I could always go back to the playground later.

He shook his head. "I can't right now. Too much work. Maybe someday I'll have time. Don't let me hold you up."

I jogged to the playground and headed for the monkey bars. All the way there, my gut bounced in front of me like a living creature trying to escape from captivity. I climbed the monkey bars and hung upside down. I even pressed on my stomach with both hands. I didn't have any luck.

"I guess I'll have to go with my backup plan," I told Mookie that afternoon when we were hanging out at his place.

"Leave the country?" he asked.

"No. Just skip the demonstration," I said.

"You're going to get in big trouble with Mr. Lomux," he said. "You're his big success story."

"I'd rather get in trouble than get snapped into pieces," I said.

"You're right. Besides, no matter what anyone else does around Mr. Lomux, I seem to get in the most trouble. He'll probably yell at me for something tonight."

I couldn't argue with that. "You do seem to be able to get him angry."

Mookie shrugged. "It's just one of my many talents."

We hung out at his place until I headed home for dinner.

After we ate—well, after my folks ate and I pushed my stuffed peppers around and cut them up until it looked like I'd eaten some of them—my dad said, "Better get ready, champ."

"For what?" I looked at the clock. I had no idea what he was talking about.

"The wrestling demonstration," he said.

"I'm not—I didn't—how'd you—?" I clamped my

mouth on the stream of babble as I tried to figure out what was going on.

"Your gym teacher called the other day," Mom said.

"He told us what a star you are in class," Dad said.

"We're so excited about the demonstration," Mom said. "He's saving your match for last."

"My son, the champ," Dad said. "Go grab your stuff."

As I climbed the stairs, I realized my mind felt as numb as my body. There was no way this evening was going to end well.

20

A Leak in the News

I called Abigail and told her what was happening.

"I'll meet you there. Maybe we can think of something."

"I hope so. Otherwise, the wrestling demonstration is going to turn into a science lesson, starring the breakaway boy." I hung up, then stuffed my shorts and sneakers into my gym bag.

"Let's go, champ," Dad said when I got back downstairs.

I followed my parents to the car and thought about faking a sudden stomachache. But I was still terrified that mom would drag me to Dr. Scrivella if I acted sick.

Maybe Rodney won't show up, I thought as Dad backed out of the driveway.

Yeah, right. He was so eager to have his shot at me, he'd get there even if he had scoot to the gym on his butt through five miles of broken glass and thumbtacks.

"You know your father wrestled in high school," Mom said.

"It was just one year," Dad said. "No big deal. But I'm glad my son is following in my footsteps."

No pressure there. I leaned back in my seat and stared out the window. Dad switched on the radio. It was set to one of those news stations.

"We have a major incident to report at a government storage facility in Exley Township," the announcer said.

Oh, no. I slunk down in my seat. Exley wasn't far from here.

"Firefighters arriving at the scene after a small exhaust-fan fire triggered an alarm discovered several barrels of chemicals that had begun to leak. Local authorities called in the FBI, which confirmed that the chemicals, when combined, form a type of nerve gas. A bit of gas had already leaked. Not enough to harm people, but some small animals and birds were already affected."

I thought about the birds and cat I'd seen flying into walls or falling out of trees.

"But here's the strangest part," the announcer said.

It gets stranger?

"According to government records, the building was

supposed to be empty. It appears someone else had been using it for storage. Authorities are investigating."

I had a feeling I knew who that "someone else" was. *There are organizations that want to destroy our society.* That's what Mr. Murphy had told me. It looked like one of them had been using the building. Maybe the same organization that had given Abigail's uncle the corpse flower. Whoever it was, they were pretty bold, and pretty clever, picking a hiding place like that.

I listened to the rest of the story. "A hazardous waste disposal team arrived at the scene last night and removed the chemicals. According to a spokesperson, the stockpile was just days, or possibly hours, away from releasing a large toxic cloud."

I thought about my friends and my parents staggering around like those birds, cats, and dogs. That would have been awful. It looked like I'd had a chance to do something good with my zombie abilities before I got broken into little pieces. I didn't know why Mr. Murphy hadn't just picked up the phone and told someone about the chemicals. But I was starting to see that the world was a lot more complicated place for spies than it was for fifth-graders. Either way, I'd done something good. I'd been a hero.

Somehow, that thought didn't cheer me up all that much. Not when I was facing the possibility that I'd be exposed as a zombie in front of a couple hundred of my neighbors. I didn't want people treating me like I was different—or running away and screaming at the sight of me.

All too soon, we reached the high school. The parking lot was mobbed. I guess a lot of people were there for the regular match, but plenty of others came for the demonstration. I saw some of my classmates climbing out of their parents' cars, carrying gym bags. They looked happy. No reason for them not to be. They were going to have an easy time tonight.

"We'll be up there in the bleachers, cheering for you," Mom said when we reached the gym.

"Go get 'em, champ!" Dad said.

I waved at them and headed across the gym. *Last chance.* I looked over my shoulder at the nearest exit. I could run off and vanish into the woods. Unlike other runaways, I wouldn't have to worry about finding food or staying warm. I'd just have to worry about ants eating my feet when I wasn't paying attention.

I walked through the double doors that led to the boys' locker room.

"Abercrombie!" Mr. Lomux said when I got inside. "Good to see you. People are going to remember this night. I promise you that."

Rodney was in the locker room, too. He only said two words to me.

"You're dead."

But he said them a couple dozen times. I swear, if I hadn't been so worried about getting my bones snapped in pieces, I would have tackled him right there. I honestly wasn't afraid of him. Even if he was strong and tough, I was willing to wrestle him. If I could face a burning house or climb an electric fence, I could face a hulking ape who thought he could get whatever he wanted by scaring people.

I left the locker room and walked over to the area of the bleachers where the wrestlers from our class were supposed to sit. I could see my parents at the top of the other bleachers, across the gym.

"Any sign of Abigail?" I asked Mookie as I plopped down next to him.

"Not yet. She's probably figuring something out."

"I hope she figures it out soon."

I heard shouting and giggles. Shawna and a bunch of other girls from our class ran out in front of us and started performing a cheering routine. It looked like something they'd thrown together at the last minute. Some of them had pom-poms. Some of them just waved their hands. But they all had matching skirts and sweaters.

Past them, I saw Abigail rush into the gym. I got up to talk to her.

"Sit!" Mr. Lomux said. "The team stays together. No wandering. You're a warrior now. Warriors need to stay focused." He turned and shouted at a kid from another class who was coming over to say hi. "Restricted. Athletes and cheerleaders."

I looked across the gym at Abigail. Whatever plan she had, there was no way I could learn it now. Mr. Lomux would never let me leave the bleachers.

21

▼

A Brilliant Plan

I guess Abigail realized I couldn't go talk to her. She went to the side of the gym, grabbed a mop from the closet, and unscrewed the head.

"What's she doing?" Mookie asked.

"I think she's sneaking over," I said.

It looked like I was right. Though I guess *sneaking* wasn't the best description.

"Go, Ravens!" Abigail screamed. She ran toward us, waving the mop head like a pompom. When she was about ten feet away from me and Mookie, she dropped the mop head and did a cartwheel. Then she leaped in the air. As she was flying toward us, I saw her move her mouth, forming the words, "Catch me!"

Mookie and I shot up from our seats and put our hands out. Abigail landed in our arms. I looked down at her. "I didn't know you could tumble."

"Ohmygosh. Neither did I. I told myself it's just simple physics."

"Like riding a bike?" I asked

She nodded and took a deep breath. I looked around. Nobody was paying any attention to us yet. That wasn't surprising. Abigail was invisible to Shawna and the rest of that group of girls.

"Better hurry, before you get kicked out," I said. "What's the plan?"

Abigail rolled off our arms. "It's simple. Your's is the last match. Right before you wrestle, I'll turn off all the power at the main circuit breaker. The gym will go dark. There are emergency lights, but they aren't very powerful. They'll cancel the rest of the demonstration and everyone will go home."

"Why not do it now?" I asked.

She shook her head. "They'd probably figure out the problem and just turn the power back on. They want the match to happen. And they want the demonstration. But nobody will care about missing the last pair."

"That makes sense. Can you really kill the power?"

"No problem. I got a copy of the building plans. They're part of the public record. But I'll need help. Mookie has to boost me up to the crawl space so I can get past the locked gates. There's one match between his and yours, so we'll have just enough time."

"How do you know the order of the matches?" I asked.

"I hacked into Mr. Lomux's computer," she said.

"You're kidding."

"Of course I'm kidding. He doesn't know how to use a computer. But he wrote up a schedule. He left it sitting in his office back at school. Reading his handwriting was a lot harder than any kind of hacking."

She turned her head toward Mookie. "As soon as your match is over, go into the locker room and sneak out the side door that leads to the hall. I'll meet you there."

"I love sneaking," Mookie said.

Abigail skittered away. The regular high school match started. I had to admit, it was exciting sitting so close to the wrestlers. I really got into it and cheered for our team.

The East Craven Ravens were amazing. We won the meet without any trouble. I could actually see where wrestling would be fun. There was a lot of skill involved. Though if I had to pick a sport when I got to high school, I think it would be track. I liked running, now that I never got out of breath.

After the last match, Mr. Lomux stood up and gave a speech. It lasted about ten minutes, but could pretty much be described with three sentences.

I'm the greatest gym teacher of all time.

These kids were nothing until I got my hands on them.

This is only the beginning of the massive athletic program I have planned for our school.

Finally, he stopped talking and let us wrestle. Every match was exciting. Unless you knew everyone was faking it. One kid would do a perfect takedown. The other would do a perfect escape. Finally, as time was running out, someone would get a pin.

Adam wrestled in the fifth match. After he won, he headed for the locker room.

"Where are you going?" Mr. Lomux asked.

"The bathroom." Adam bounced from foot to foot like someone who'd had way too much milk at dinner.

Mr. Lomux pointed at the bleachers. "Sit. You stay with your team until the end."

"But . . ."

"Sit!"

Adam sat. I looked at Mookie. "How are you going to get to the locker room?"

"I don't know. I'll figure something out."

The whole time we sat there, Rodney kept looking over at me and whispering, "You're dead."

No kidding.

Finally, Mookie's turn came. He and Dilby walked out onto the mat. They faced each other.

"I'm going to rip you into tiny pieces!" Mookie shouted. He clenched his fists like the wrestlers on TV. "I'll tear you up! I'll mutilate you!"

Dilby stared at Mookie. He was obviously totally confused. He stuck a finger in his ear and rooted around for wax.

Mookie turned toward the bleachers. "I'm Mookasaurus! Fear me!"

"Stop that!" Mr. Lomux shouted.

Mookie thrust his thumb at his chest. "I'm the champion of the world! I'm the greatest wrestler that ever lived! Mooka-saurus! Mooka-saurus! Moo-ka-sau-rus!" He stuck both hands out, palms up, and lifted them in the air with each shout, like he was trying to get the crowd to chant along.

Mr. Lomux walked over to Mookie and yelled, "Get out."

Mookie pointed at Mr. Lomux's head. "Nine veins! Yes! It's a new record. The Mookasaurus is Mooka-awesome."

"OUT!!!" Mr. Lomux screamed. I could see the tenth vein from all the way across the mat.

"Okay. Sure." Mookie dashed toward the locker room.

"You have detention for the rest of the year!" Mr. Lomux called after him.

As Mookie slipped through the door, Mr. Lomux turned toward the crowd. "No problem, folks. There's one bad apple in every bunch. But we have two more matches for you, and I think you're going to be totally thrilled by the final one."

I watched the next pair—Omar and Mort—wrestle. When it was my turn, Rodney leaped off the bench like he'd been sitting on a spring, and raced onto the mat. I guess he couldn't wait to start shredding me like a wet napkin.

I got up from the bleachers and walked toward the mat as slowly as I could. Across the mat, I saw my dad give me a thumbs-up. In the front row, I saw some guys in suits and some women in nice dresses and pearl neck-laces. *School board*, I thought. Definitely not your average group of wrestling fans.

I reached the mat. The gym lights were still on. How much more time did Abigail need? I knelt and retied my left sneaker. Then I retied the right one. I reached for the left sneaker again.

"Let's go," Mr. Lomux said.

I walked onto the mat, crouched, and faced Rodney.

22

▼

An Unpleasant Outcome

I thought about trying to shoot for a takedown. If I got a quick pin, it would all be over. I
really believed I could beat Rodney by using skill.
Wrestling wasn't about strength. It was about balance
and leverage. Okay, my balance wasn't great right now,
but I still felt I could beat him.

But if I messed up, something would break. Maybe a
lot of things. My safest bet was to lose as quickly as possible. I knew Dad would be disappointed if I lost, but I
think he'd be more disappointed if my foot flew off my
leg and knocked out somebody's eye.

The only problem was, even if I let Rodney win, he'd
try to hurt me.

The lights were still on.

"You're dead," Rodney whispered.

"There are worse things," I said.

The referee blew his whistle.

"I'm gonna break your legs," Rodney said. "And then I'm gonna rip your ears off."

No way. I'm not a victim. I made a split-second decision to try for a pin. I knew I could put Rodney flat on his back. I was going to take him down, big-time. That would definitely make me a hero to all the kids in school.

I took a step, then staggered as I lost my balance.

Before I could recover, Rodney dove forward and wrapped his arms around both my legs. With a grunt, he lifted me straight up. I felt like I was on a carnival ride. Then he slammed me down on my back. Instead of coming down with me to the mat, he dropped me, then leaped in the air.

Rodney fell toward me like a meteor.

He body-slammed me in the gut with all his weight.

At that instant, the lights went out.

So did something else.

When Rodney slammed into my stomach, my head tilted back and everything in my gut jetted out through my throat like soda pop from a bottle that had been shaken really hard. The food got pushed both by Rodney's weight and by all the gas that had built up inside me.

It felt like my mouth had turned into a hose nozzle. From the way it sounded, some of the stream caught Rodney right in the face. He got knocked off me. It sounded like the rest landed in the bleachers. That was followed by another sound—unlike anything I could have imagined.

It can't be, I thought.

I saw flickers of light straight above me and off to the sides. The emergency lights were kicking in.

WHOOMPH!

A dazzling flash over my head lit the room for an instant. Abigail had warned me about explosive gas. The gas cloud must have drifted straight up, and been set off by the nearest light. The two lights on the side walls had survived. They were dim, but they were bright enough so I could see what was happening in the bleachers. And I could see where the sound came from.

All around the gym, people were bending over, gagging, and throwing up. Those who hadn't thrown up right away joined in when they got splattered from behind.

The bleachers had turned into a fountain of puke.

Anyone who wasn't throwing up was holding his nose. People streamed out of the gym. I guess the mess of liquefied wings I'd cooked up in my gut smelled pretty awful.

I took a short sniff through my nose. Not short enough. Wow. I stopped as soon as the amazing foulness of the odor hit me. It made one of Mookie's sauerkraut farts seem as pleasant as roses and cinnamon. The people of East Craven might have been saved from the toxic fumes of the leaking chemicals, but they'd definitely gotten a dose of something almost as bad.

Shawna and the rest of the girls ran past me, screaming. They looked like they'd lost a mud fight. The *eeeks* and *eeewws* got muffled when they escaped into the locker room, but I had a feeling they'd be shuddering for the rest of the night. If not longer.

Mr. Lomux was on his knees. Every couple seconds, he hunched over, jerked like he'd been zapped by an electric fence, and added to the splattered mess on the floor. I guess he had a weak stomach. After a while, he crawled on his hands and knees toward the locker room.

I was still on my back. I sat up and looked around. Rodney was sprawled out a couple feet away, clutching his face and moaning. It looked like he'd taken a pretty heavy hit. He got up and staggered away.

"You okay, champ?"

I looked over at Dad. His face was pale, but I guess he'd managed not to throw up on his clothes.

"I'm fine. I just need to catch my breath." I looked past him at Mom. She seemed okay. I think moms are tougher than the rest of us. They have to deal with babies, and there really isn't anything grosser and smellier than that. I waved at her to let her know I was okay.

Dad glanced over his shoulder. "Must have been some kind of gas leak. I guess it made a lot of people sick. Whatever it was, it knocked out the lights, too."

"Yeah. That was something, all right." I spotted Mookie and Abigail coming down the hall. They both froze by the door. I guess they didn't want to step inside the gym and face the full force of the stinking air. "Dad, do you mind if I walk home with my friends?"

"Not at all." He started to leave, then turned back and said, "I'm sorry you didn't get a chance to wrestle tonight."

"That's okay."

"He was big, but I think you could have taken him."

"Yeah. I think I could. I've got a better sense of balance."

Dad and Mom left. I climbed to my feet and checked my balance. I was definitely doing better now that my stomach wasn't bulging over my pants. That was good. I took careful steps toward Mookie and Abigail as they waited for me by the door.

"Good work, you two. Thanks."

"You're alive," Mookie said.

"Yeah."

"And in one piece," Abigail said.

"Not exactly."

They both stared at me. I pointed to my left leg. "I think it broke."

"But you're walking," Mookie said.

"I'm sort of balancing on it. The skin didn't tear all the way off, but I definitely have to glue the bone back. It snapped. I didn't feel it, but I heard it, for sure." I turned my head, being careful not to lean too far, and looked at my calf. I could see a rip along the back side of my leg. I felt my head. Everything was still attached. At least Rodney didn't get a chance to tear my ears off.

"Got your glue?" Mookie asked.

I pointed to the locker room. "I got a ton. It's in my bag."

Mookie ran off for the bag.

"Come on, Humpty Dumpty, let's go find a quiet room where we can glue you back together," Abigail said after Mookie returned.

They got on either side of me and I put my arms around them. I shuffled down the high school hallway, between my two friends.

"You're going to have to help me glue this," I said. "I can't reach."

"No problem," Mookie said.

"It's going to be pretty gross," I warned him.

"Cool," Mookie said.

"And fascinating," Abigail said.

"I hate to say it," I told them, "but I realized something as I was lying on the mat."

"I think I know what you're going to tell us," Abigail said.

"You're going to become a wrestler?" Mookie asked. "Awesome. I'll be your manager."

"No. Something far scarier," I said. "I'm going to become an agent for BUM."

"Why?" he asked.

"They're the only ones might be able to keep my bones from breaking. The machine doesn't work, yet. But they're still my best hope. And it seems like they really are doing some good things. They exposed those toxic chemicals before anyone got hurt. And they're trying to stop the people who are giving kids dangerous things like those chemistry sets." I looked at Abigail. "You understand, don't you?"

"Sure. I understand. You're definitely doing good things. I heard about that building on the news, and figured out the connection. It was fiendishly clever of the bad guys to hide their chemicals in one of the government's empty buildings. There would have been a disaster if you hadn't done something. But that's not the only reason you want to join BUM. It's not just about doing good things, is it?"

"Nope. I guess it's kind of exciting, too. Driving around in the dark, sneaking into places, beating the bad guys. I mean, I'm going to be a real spy. And they have a lot of cool stuff to play with."

"Even if most of it explodes," Mookie said.

"Especially if most of it explodes," I said.

In some ways, I guess spies were almost as cool as superheroes. As a superhero, I could save one person at a time. As I spy, I'd already saved hundreds. Maybe thousands. So what if they'd never know? I knew. That's all that mattered.

I touched my chest. "I might be dead, but being a spy really makes me feel alive."

Later

I got online that night and logged in to *Vampyre Stalker*. Instead of waiting for Peter Plowshare to come to me, I went up the hill and had my battle with Nastydamus. It was tough, but I won. As I left the crypt, I found myself face-to-face with a peasant.

Staker Slaymaster: *What took you so long?*

Peter Plowshare: *I figured you'd like a chance to have the battle I'd interrupted. Nice job with the garlic and holy water. He never had a chance.*

Staker Slaymaster: *Thanks.*

Peter Plowshare: *So, are you joining us?*

Staker Slaymaster: *Yeah. I want to make the world a better place.*

Peter Plowshare: *Good. And you shall. I'll have an important mission for you soon.*

He walked off before I could ask anything. *An important mission.* That sounded cool.

I still didn't completely trust Mr. Murphy. But at least I had Abigail and Mookie on my side. I'd trust them with my life. Or death.

Dad wasn't the only one who believed the whole thing in the gym was caused by some sort of gas leak that blew out the lights and sickened everyone. The newspaper ran a story about a mystery gas. Nobody seemed to remember that the lights went out before the explosion. According to Abigail, eyewitness reports are often wrong.

Denali's parents got a ton of business at their dry-cleaning shop. She said they picked up a lot of new customers. People really appreciated that they were open late. Especially on Saturday night. Business was so good, they hired extra workers.

Mr. Lomux was out for a while on sick leave, so Mookie didn't have to do any detention. By the time Mr. Lomux came back, I'm sure he'd have forgotten about it. The substitute gym teacher, Mr. Svengal, was great. The high school gym was closed for a week while they cleaned it and tried to get rid of the smell.

I wasn't planning to enter any more eating contests. Though I'm sure Mookie would dream up other ways I could make money. He really thought I should try video game competitions. That definitely sounded safer. And I could get in tons of practice at night.

So, in a lot of ways, it wasn't a perfect week for me. But it wasn't all bad. Especially at the end of the week. I went downstairs a bit after sunrise on Sunday morning. Dad was waiting for me, wearing sweatclothes and sneakers. "I was hoping you'd be up early," he said. "Mind if I join you?"

"That would be great. You're not too tired?"

"You know, I think I had more energy when I used to run. It's worth a try. And it's a good chance to spend some time together."

We headed out for a run. We talked a little, too. But not too much. It was nice. I think Dad liked it as much as I did.

"You going to stick with wrestling?" he asked as we headed up the hill toward the park.

"I think I like this better," I said.

"Me, too. So, anything interesting happening in your life?"

"The usual fifth-grade stuff," I said.

"Matters of life and death?" Dad asked, flashing me a grin.

"Exactly."

TURN THE PAGE
FOR A SNEAK PEEK AT

GOOP
SOUP

Nathan Abercrombie,
Accidental Zombie
—————— BOOK THREE

1

Stool Pigeon

When the pigeon shot into our classroom, most of the boys shouted, "Whoa!" About half the girls shouted, "Eewwww!"

Our teacher, Ms. Delambre, shouted, "My goodness!"

That's the sort of thing adults say when they're trying not to use bad words. My friend Mookie and I grinned at each other. His mom says *My goodness* a lot.

I didn't shout anything until the pigeon swooped down from the ceiling and landed on my left shoulder.

"Hey! Get off!"

It didn't.

I reached up to push it away, but I was afraid I might hurt it. I read somewhere that birds have hollow bones. I knew how that felt. My own bones break pretty easily.

They weren't always like that. I was a normal kid until

I got splashed with Hurt-Be-Gone and turned into a half-dead zombie by my friend Abigail's crazy Uncle Zardo. Now, I don't have a heartbeat. But, much to my surprise, that hasn't been too big a problem.

The pigeon turned its head and stared at me.

I stared back.

The pigeon blinked.

I didn't.

That's another thing I don't need to do. Though I try to remember to make myself blink once in a while so I don't creep people out.

The pigeon's tail twitched. Something wet and white plopped on my shirt, right across my pocket.

"Great. Thanks a lot," I told the pigeon.

I'd just been turned into a living statue. What next? Maybe the pigeon would build a nest in my hair and lay eggs.

As kids all around me collapsed in laughter, pointed at my shirt, and made bad jokes about pigeon poop, the bird fluttered off my shoulder and swooped back out the window.

Mookie, who was sitting next to me, laughed so hard he fell off his stool. And he fell so hard, he bounced. I guess he didn't get hurt, because he kept laughing.

Only Abigail wasn't laughing. She turned toward the window, watched the pigeon, and tugged at the ends of her frizzy, dark brown hair. She's so smart, it's almost scary. But she never shows off in school.

"All right, class!" Ms. Delambre said. "That's quite

enough. Settle down. This is science class—not party time." She walked over to me and pointed at the blotch on my shirt. "Nathan, go wash that off immediately. Pigeon droppings carry all sorts of diseases."

I hopped down from my stool and headed for the sink in the back of the room. I could feel two dozen pairs of eyes following me. I wasn't worried about germs. I was pretty sure I couldn't get any kind of disease. And even if I did, it couldn't hurt me. But I still didn't want that stuff on my shirt. Mom is always telling me to be careful about getting food on my clothes. If she ever sat through a lunch period in the school cafeteria, she'd know how impossible that is.

I grabbed a paper towel and wiped at the stain. I expected the blob to smear. But it stuck to the paper towel and slid right off my pocket.

What in the world . . . ?

I realized it was a piece of plastic. There was something printed on the back side in tiny letters. I looked closer.

Urgent mission coming. Major operation. Be ready to spring into action. P.M.

P.M. That had to be Peter Murphy—the spy who'd recruited me to work for the Bureau of Useful Misadventures. BUM looks for kids who mess up in some kind of way that makes them good spies. They also fight to make the world a better place. That's their mission, though I'm still not sure exactly what it means.

I crumpled up the paper towel and tossed it in the trash. Urgent mission? Cool. That was exciting, and also a little scary. I was going to get my first real spy assignment from BUM. Nathan Abercrombie, Super Spy. This is the job I was born for. Or died for, I guess.

I returned to our lab table. Mookie had climbed back onto his stool, but he was still choking down snorts and spitting out chuckles. He sounded like a steam engine that was in danger of exploding—a short, round steam engine with large, square glasses and shaggy light brown hair.

"It's not that funny," I said.

He shook his head. "It's more than funny. It's like mega-funny. No, giga-funny. Wait—what comes after giga?"

"Tera," Abigail said.

"Tera-funny?" Mookie frowned, then said it a couple more times, like he was trying to taste the words. "Nope. Sounds too serious. I'll stick with giga-funny, 'cause that sounds like giggles. And seeing Nate get splattered really makes me giggle." He started laughing again.

Abigail tapped my arm. "I assume the pigeon was delivering a message from BUM." She and Mookie were the only people who knew about my secret life as a soon-to-be spy. The other kids in school didn't even know I was a zombie. To them I was just plain old Nathan Abercrombie, the second-skinniest kid in class.

"Yeah. They have a mission for me. Something big. How'd you know it wasn't a real bird?"

"Wing speed and movement," Abigail said. "Real pigeons don't fly that way. They don't crash and burn, either. That one flew smack into the phone pole." She pointed out the window.

I leaned toward the window and spotted the smoldering remains of the mechanical bird on the street.

"Why can't they just call me on the phone or send an e-mail?" I asked. BUM loved using all sorts of robots and high-tech equipment. It didn't seem to bother them that most of it blew up or caught on fire.

Abigail sighed. "Boys and their toys. Even when they grow up, they have to play."

"Well, yeah," I said. "Toys are cool."

Mookie stopped laughing and poked my shoulder. He opened his mouth to say something, then lost control again.

"Just say it," I told him. I was getting tera-tired of this.

"Are you exhausted?" he asked.

"You know I don't need to sleep." That was actually the best part about being half-dead—I could stay up all night and play computer games. Or do other things—if I ever figured out something better to do.

"But you must be really really really exhausted," he said.

I didn't want to ask, but he was my best friend, and I could tell he was dying to do this. "Okay, why do you think I'm exhausted?"

"Because you look POOPED!"

He fell off his stool again.

"Are you finished?" I asked as we headed outside for recess.

"I'm not sure. I mean, you have to admit it's pretty funny."

167

"Hilarious," I said. "But maybe it's time to drop it."

"Drop!" He pointed at my shirt, then started laughing again. "The pigeon already dropped it!"

He was like that for the rest of the day. All through recess, he kept grabbing the ends of his jacket and stretching his arms out, making wings. "I'm MookieHawk!" he shouted. "Don't mess with me, or I'll mess your shirt." He'd flap his arms a couple times, race over to me, scream *PLOP!*, and then fall down laughing.

By the end of recess, he must have fallen about twenty times. But that was okay. Even though he kept kidding me, I was happy the rest of the day, thinking about my first spy mission.

At least, I was happy until that evening, when Mom hit me with the worst possible news a half-dead zombie kid could hear.

WRITING AND RESEARCH ACTIVITIES

I. Spies Like You?

A. Nathan's "zombie" gifts have lined him up for recruitment into the spy world. Imagine you are Dr. Cushing. Write a short report to Mr. Murphy, noting the qualities you observe in Nathan and how they might be applied to spy work. Wearing a lab coat, present your report to friends or classmates.

B. Go to the library or online to learn about famous spies and espionage campaigns from history, such as Sir Francis Walsingham, Nathan Hale, members of the Duquesne Spy Ring, the Cambridge Spy Ring, "Major Martin" (Operation Mincemeat), or Sir William Samuel Stephenson ("Intrepid"). Based on your report, draw a portrait or scene featuring your chosen spy/group. Mount your drawing on a larger piece of colored paper and fill the margins with facts about your spy's identity, career, and honors or punishments, if applicable. Combine your project with those of classmates to create a "Wall of Spies" display.

C. Learn more about the United States Intelligence Community, starting with a visit to http://www.intelligence.gov/1-members.shtml. Make an outline describing the various agencies with intelligence roles. Conclude with a paragraph noting whether you would like to work in intelligence and, if so, with which agency you would most like a job.

D. Would you make a good spy? What unusual qualities do you have that might help you do your job? Write a letter to BUM explaining why you would make a great recruit. Read your letter aloud to friends or classmates.

E. Individually or in small groups, create a spy organization. Draw your spy lab on graph paper, labeling equipment, experiment stations and features, and explain how you would get to the lab's hidden location.

Write a mission statement describing your goals and/or responsibilities. Design a logo for your agency.

II. Brittle Bones and Other Problems
with Being Undead

A. Finding a cure for his brittle bones is a key reason Nathan considers working with BUM. In the character of Nathan, make a list of the challenges of living with brittle bones. Are there any advantages? If so, list and describe them.

B. In chapter 5, Nathan mentions that reading about Edgar Allan Poe makes him feel as though his own life is sort of normal. Read a short story by Poe and research his life. Write a short essay describing Poe's contributions to mystery and suspense literature. Or, with classmates or friends, divide into groups to debate whether Poe's life was better or worse than Nathan's.

C. Imagine that you, like Nathan, do not have to sleep, eat, and/or breathe. Write a short (3–5 page) story in which this characteristic proves to be a great benefit or a great liability for you.

D. As a local reporter, write a newspaper or website article describing the nauseating events that took place at the high school wrestling demonstration. Then, with classmates or friends, role-play a conversation between Nathan, Abigail, and Mookie in which they react to the report's misinformation and joke about what really happened.

III. Friends and Fighters

A. Abigail and Mookie both have qualities that make them great friends to Nathan. Write a paragraph describing Abigail's qualities as a friend, then another describing Mookie's friendship traits. Write a final paragraph describing whether you are an Abigail-type or a Mookie-type of friend and why.

B. Throughout the novel, Nathan and his classmates engage in bouts of fake wrestling. Go to the library or online to learn more about scholastic wrestling at such sites as the National Federation of State High School Association's wrestling page (http://www.nfhs.org/

Activity2.aspx?id-2782). Record a "radio broadcast" describing a fake wrestling match. Or, use animation software or stop-motion animation techniques to create a short cartoon about a fake wrestling tournament.

C. The novel is peppered with Internet dialogues between Staker Slaymaster (Nathan) and Peter Plowshare. Go to the library or online to learn about the expression "swords into plowshares." Write an essay describing what clues this expression may offer as to whether Nathan should consider the people of the BUM agency enemies or friends.

QUESTIONS FOR DISCUSSION

1. As the novel begins, how do Nathan and his friends Abigail and Mookie realize that someone is spying on Nathan? What concerns does this realization cause each of these characters? What would you worry about if you felt you were being spied upon?

2. List and describe the workings of funny gadgets employed by BUM, such as the "squirrel-cam." How do these gadgets affect your impressions of the agency? If you could invent an unusual spy device, what would you create and why?

3. In chapter 5, Mookie says, "I never thought hanging out with a dead guy could get you killed." Chapter 7's title, "A Sock in the Face," has an amusing double meaning. What other wordplays and puns does the author use in the course of the story? What, in your opinion, is the funniest chapter in the novel?

4. How is Nathan partly responsible for Mr. Lomux's new plan to turn the class into star wrestlers? Why is Nathan better able to endure Mr. Lomax's "toughening up" exercises than the other kids? How does he help the class solve the problem of being made to wrestle one another?

5. In chapter 8, Nathan describes Mr. Lomux as "a loser who suddenly got a taste of victory." How does this make him dangerous? Do other characters in the novel fit this description and, if so, how does it affect their attitudes or behavior? Is it always bad for losers to get a "taste of victory"?

6. What role does the Internet play in the novel? Would you have advised Nathan to continue to play *Vampyre Stalker*? Why or why not? What restrictions or considerations are part of your own Internet use? Are such limits important?

7. Mr. Murphy subjects Nathan to some tests that seem a lot like tricks. How would you have reacted to these tests? Do you think Nathan's assessment of Dr. Cushing is correct? How might you suggest Mr. Murphy test Nathan's loyalty? What might you suggest Nathan do to try to get to the truth about BUM?

8. How does Mookie propose Nathan get the money they need for Abigail to create a bone-strengthening machine? Is this plan successful? What unexpected problem does it cause? How does Abigail explain the scientific situation?

9. In chapter 13, Ms. Otranto asks her students to consider: "What does it mean to make a sacrifice for someone else?" How would you answer this question? How might this question be of use to Nathan as he considers becoming a spy?

10. In the introduction to *Dead Guy Spy*, Nathan comments that he "used to think secret agents were these awesome guys who drove fast cars, wore expensive clothes, and practiced deadly karate. Now I know better." What has Nathan learned? Has his experience changed the way you imagine secret agents or your thoughts about how to decide when to trust an individual or organization? Explain your answer.

11. At the end of the novel, Nathan finds a new connection with his dad through running. How did being a zombie actually help lead him to this connection? Have you ever been surprised by the way an interest or activity has helped you form a new relationship with a parent, friend, or other member of your community? What are some good things about making connections through shared interests?

12. At the end of the story, what is your opinion of BUM? What do you think is the main reason Nathan decides to join up with BUM? If you were asked, would you work with the agency? Why or why not?